Happy reading, Jayo! ☺

Corrina Austin

Corrina Austin

Mar 31/18

DANCING LEMUR PRESS, L.L.C.
Pikeville, North Carolina
www.dancinglemurpress.com

Dedication

For Lucy, who has always been in my corner.

Acknowledgements

Heartfelt thanks to Robyn Walker, who is always there to fan the embers when the fire is about to go out.

To the family and friends who took time to read the first draft of "Corners" and offer feedback and encouragement, you are deeply appreciated.

Table of Contents

Chapter One..7

Chapter Two...17

ChapterThree...27

Chapter Four...37

Chapter Five...46

Chapter Six..52

Chapter Seven..66

Chapter Eight..76

Chapter Nine...88

ChapterTen..100

Chapter Eleven..112

Chapter Twelve..124

August, 1969

The first time I laid eyes on Ellis Wynne, it was through the burn of a chlorine haze, and I was spewing water all over the concrete deck of the public swimming pool. I was ten years old that summer.

Other kids my age had already swum twice across the width of the deep-end—the requirement to graduate out of the shallow end. Halfway through public swim, the lifeguards would raise their whistles to their lips and blast them in unison, and all the swimmers scrambled out of the pool. The ones who strived to earn deep water privileges lined up down at the deep end, shivering in their wet bathing suits, hugging themselves. Everyone else settled on their wet towels to watch the show.

A lifeguard in a pair of dark sunglasses and a red Speedo (a tight one-piece for the young ladies, and for the guys, a tiny suit that looked more like a pair of too-small briefs than swimwear) would take the long rescue pole from its perch on the fence and nod to the first swimmer in line. The kid would stand on the edge of the pool, toes curled over the lip of white concrete, squeeze his or her nose between thumb and forefinger, and drop into the water. Up would bob a gasping wet head and off the kid would thrash, inching his or her way across the deep end. The lifeguard held the pole within reach, in the event of panic—or worse, failure. A kid could swim any stroke of preference—breaststroke, front crawl, dog paddle, or absurd combination thereof—anything that propelled a body across the pool. Once the other side was attained, there was no lingering there. Touch the edge, then turn and head back for the second lap. Sometimes, the kid, either blinded by chlorine or eyes screwed shut, would veer away from the edge towards the middle of the pool. The lifeguard would give his whistle a little toot, and the wretched swimmer would flounder back, as though trying to locate a lifeboat in fog. The audience on towels would applaud successful attempts and collectively moan the failures.

That summer, I attempted the crossing every single day for seven weeks. I grabbed for the pole every time. And that was before I'd even made it across once. I would be dragged to the edge like a harpooned fish, a helpful hand would lower, and I would land flipping and flopping on the deck for all to see and pity.

I watched the kids that made the crossings pin their deep-end medallions onto their bathing suits, their dripping faces glowing. When the whistle blasted again to signal everyone back into the pool, those kids would plunge triumphantly into water over their heads and then get out and line up at the ultimate symbol of public pool prestige—the diving board. I'd slink back to the shallow end and resume my repetitive swimming along the rope that marked the fortress between the deep and the shallow. I'd swim back and forth, back and forth, almost without effort. When I knew I could touch the bottom without my head going under the water, I had no problem. But when I knew the water could close over my head and my feet had nothing to stand on, it was like my body turned to stone. Panic sank me, every time.

That day, after weeks of failure, I was desperate. The whistles would blow and everyone would climb out of the pool. I would be in that miserable line again.

The lifeguard would give me an encouraging word. Or worse, a pitying glance. I needed to face the deep end on my own terms, with no one watching. I dipped beneath the water and resurfaced on the other side of the rope.

It was still shallow. I could stand there, which I did, for quite some time. The lifeguards sat in their tall chairs or paced the perimeter of the deck. No one noticed that I had traversed into forbidden territory. I edged out a little further. I can do this, I told myself.

And then, my feet shot out from under me. I skied down the slanted bottom of the pool. Water closed abruptly over my head.

My mother had somehow scrambled money together for swimming lessons for me. She might not be able to pay for hockey or piano lessons or Boy Scouts, but she could sure as fire find some money somewhere for swimming lessons. She'd never had them as a child and couldn't swim a stroke. I'd had two weeks of instruction for the past three summers. I could float, I could scull, I could crawl, so long as I was in the safety of shallow water.

However, my mother's investment in my water safety had apparently not yielded any kind of return when it came to the deep end. There I was, at the bottom of the pool, and showing no signs of floating to the top. I cannot describe even now how quickly resigned I was to my inevitable death at the tender age of ten.

But then, moving sylph-like through the depths, a shimmering form appeared in front of me, framed in a cascade of swirling dark hair. In my panic, I surmised that it was the Angel of Death or something akin to that, arriving to mercifully hasten my departure. Luminous arms reached through the bubbles that streamed from my mouth and nostrils. Grasped under the shoulders, I was pulled up and away into the brilliant light and the blessed air. Whistles blasted and kids were evacuating the pool. I was dragged up onto the deck, sputtering and gagging. Still alive.

"Are you alright?" someone was saying. It was Mike, the head lifeguard. "Keep those kids back, Holly," he told the other guard who crouched there beside him.

"Stay back!" Holly shouted at the throng of kids crowding up. "Everything is fine!" Obviously, this generic form of reassurance did nothing to convince the hordes. A sea of dripping, gaggling faces was spread above me as I lay flat on my back.

I sat up, massaging my eye sockets with my knuckles. All three lifeguards were balanced on their haunches, clustered around me. Standing directly behind them was a young girl in a green bathing suit with dripping, long brown hair. She looked down calmly, regarding me with solemn grey eyes, gathering her wet hair into a rope and twisting the water out of it.

"Can you talk?" Mike asked me.

"Yes."

"What were you doing in the deep end?" he demanded.

I looked down. "I think I'm going to throw up," I blurted.

"I'm not surprised. You probably swallowed half the pool. What happened?"

"I just...I just wanted to practice, without everybody looking at me."

Mike shook his head. "That was stupid, Davy. Really stupid. You almost drowned. You would have, if this girl here hadn't noticed you were in trouble. Get your stuff and go home. You're banned from the pool for the rest of the summer. And from day camp, too. I'll call your mother tonight."

It was 1969, and stupid was a perfectly

acceptable word for adults to use with kids back then. When children screwed up, no-one draped an arm across their shoulders and gently referred to the misdemeanour as a bad choice or an inappropriate decision. They called it what it was. Which was, in my case, stupid.

Mike looked at me with abject disappointment, then stood and moved away. He had been my swimming instructor that summer, and I'd really liked him. My teachers at school had been women up until that time, and I'd never had a dad. Being taught and encouraged by Mike had been a great experience for me. Losing his approval stung hard.

The lifeguards blasted their whistles. Everyone turned away from me and jumped back into the pool.

I got to my feet, and noticed the girl who had saved me was still standing there, now quietly toweling her long, wet hair.

"Thanks," I said. "Really. Thanks a lot."

She nodded. "Do you live near here?"

"Yeah," I said. "Guess I better go, since I am now banished from the pool."

"I'll walk with you," the girl said. "You look kind of green."

"All right," I agreed.

"Meet you out front."

I went into the boys' change house and struggled into my shorts and shirt without bothering to towel off. By that point, all I wanted to do was to get away from the pool as fast as I could. The girl stood outside the entrance when I came out, leaning against the mortar-bricked wall. She'd put a bright yellow summer dress on over her suit and slid her feet into flip-flops with plastic flowers on top.

"I live that way," I told her, gesturing across the playground. "It's not too far."

"My Grammy's house is over that way, too," she

replied. "How old are you?"

"Ten. How old are you?"

"Thirteen. My name is Ellis. Not Alice. Short e. Ellis Wynne."

"I'm Davy," I replied.

"I know. I was listening when Mike chewed you out."

"Oh. Yeah." I hung my head, humiliated to think of the vast crowd present during my chastisement, listening to every word.

We headed off across the park. The sky was cloudless above us. Some lady was pushing her two kids on the baby swings nearby. They laughed and squealed, kicking their sandaled feet towards the clouds.

"I've seen you swim the rope dozens of times," Ellis said. "Why can't you make it across the deep end?"

I shrugged. "I just panic, I guess."

"Swimming in deep water is exactly the same thing as swimming in shallow water."

"I know. But I can't do it."

Ellis was quiet. "What else do you do?" she finally said. "When you're not swimming the rope."

"I don't know," I hesitated. "Well, I draw stuff, sometimes."

Ellis looked at me. "What do you draw?"

"Everything," I replied. "But I can't just sit around and draw for the next two weeks. I have to be someplace where there's adult supervision. My mom works all day; she won't let me stay home alone. That's why I'm at the pool all afternoon. It's not because I like to swim. I don't even have any friends at the pool. It's boring."

My back and shoulders itched under my T-shirt, chronic sunburn from a summer of afternoons at the pool. I fidgeted and twisted. Finally, I stopped under a tree and dragged my back along the rough bark.

"Ahhhh," I breathed.

"Where do your friends hang out?" Ellis said, leaning against the tree.

I shrugged absently. "Don't really have any friends." I didn't want Ellis to think that my social challenges bothered me overly much.

Ellis and I scuffed along the hot sidewalk. She didn't say anything encouraging or conciliatory, which I found quite satisfactory.

"Here's my house," I said. "Where does your grandmother live?"

"Just up the street a bit. I'm staying there for the summer." She peered through the tangle of bushes at the end of my driveway. "The yard looks pretty overgrown."

"My mom says Mr. Mosely doesn't do much back there," I replied. "Mr. Mosely's the landlord."

Ellis turned up the driveway. I followed her through the sagging gate into the back yard. We stood knee-deep in weeds, looking around. There were two rusty poles off to the side, holding up a sagging clothesline. The chain link fence was rusty, too, festooned with straggling vines. A large willow stood hunched in the centre. Broken branches and twigs littered the yellow grass beneath it. The outdoor fireplace was crumbling bricks, and filled with blackened cans and cigarette butts. In the back corner was an old shed, with peeling paint and dropping shingles.

"How can you play back here?" Ellis wondered.

"I don't play back here. It's creepy," I answered. "And my mother says there's broken glass."

Ellis surveyed the back of the house. The dented back screen door crouched under a tattered awning, Next to it stood a decrepit row of garbage cans, some of them toppled over and spilling potato peels and empty cans. The windows were dirty, covered on the inside with old blankets. Ellis looked at the upstairs windows. "Which bedroom is yours?" she said.

"We live in the basement," I answered.

No one had ever asked about my house before. I'd never had anyone over. The apartment was the only home I'd ever known. It had never occurred to me to be embarrassed by it. It occurred to me then.

"Can I see it?" Ellis said.

"Well..." I hesitated. "I guess you can come in. My mom's still at work. Wait here. I'll get the key."

I left Ellis scouting the perimeter of the back yard and went to the side of the house. My mother kept the key hidden in a very subtle spot—under an overturned terracotta pot. I unlocked the door and put the key back under the pot.

I gestured to Ellis and led her down the stairs.

I gave the door at the bottom a shove—it always stuck in the heat during the summer time—and we went inside.

"This is it!" I said, a little too enthusiastically. "It ain't much, but it's home." I'd heard my mother say this several times, as a way of welcome to the occasional visitors.

"It's not very big," I added.

"I like small places," Ellis replied.

"You do?" I said, doubtfully.

"Small places are cozy," Ellis said. "Show me your room."

"It's through the kitchen," I explained, leading the way. We edged past the narrow path between the white Formica table and the wall. The kitchen was cramped and dingy. The fridge turned on with a loud clunk and then a hum and a rattle as we passed. It was a noisy old thing and must have weighed as much as a car. Every few weeks my mother had to thaw out the freezer compartment, chipping away the thick walls of ice and tossing the snowy slabs into the sink. She loathed the thing, but I considered it a constant friend. The fridge kept me company through the long nights. I knew the sounds and complaints of its innards as well as I knew my own.

"This is it," I said, opening the door to my room and flicking the light switch. Ellis stepped in, and I followed closely behind.

There was one small window near the ceiling, but it didn't admit much light in the summer. The bushes grew high outside it. My bed was in the far corner. I sidled over to it and quickly shoved Boo under my pillow. Boo was the little stuffed rabbit I'd had since I was a baby. I never went to bed without him. He was grey and threadbare, eye-less for as long as I could remember.

Ellis didn't seem to notice my evasive action. She walked along the walls, looking at all my drawings. Every time I made a picture, I taped it up. It wasn't so much because I thought the drawings were any good. My bedroom walls were covered in wallpaper that had roses all over it—in various shades of luminous pink. And they were enormous. I loathed those girly roses. There wasn't a hope of new wallpaper, so the only solution was to tape things over top.

Ellis went to the desk in the corner. The desk had always been in my room—a huge, dark, cumbersome thing with claw feet and a heavy roll top that still worked. It had been in the apartment when my mother moved in, before I was born. It was too heavy to move, so Mom had just left it where it sat.

"Is this where you draw?" Ellis said.

"Yes," I said. "And do my homework and stuff."

"This desk is super neat," Ellis said. "Does it have those corners and nooks inside?"

"Yeah, lots of them," I answered. "You can roll the top up if you want to see inside it."

Ellis ran her hands over the roll-top, and then grasped the handle at the bottom and pulled it up.

Her damp dark hair fell forward, shielding her face.

"Cool," she said softly, running her fingers along the crannies and compartments.

My spirits lifted a little. I sank in deep water. Mike hated me. I lived in a crappy basement apartment and didn't have a back yard. There were pink roses all over my bedroom walls. I didn't have a dad. No one at school liked me. My mother was going to wail me out when she heard I'd been kicked out of the public pool for the rest of the summer. How was it that I could feel kind of...lucky? Astonishingly, at that moment, I did.

With that strange feeling, the full implications of what had almost happened to me at the pool began to dawn on me. If Ellis hadn't dragged me out of the deep end, I would be dead—not standing here in my rose-covered room with the fridge clunking away outside my door. If it hadn't been for Ellis, my mother would be standing in this room alone, looking at my drawings all over the walls, clutching Boo to her chest and crying herself sick. Tears jumped into my eyes.

Ellis straightened from the desk and I quickly turned around, not wanting her to see my tears.

Ellis's voice was gentle. "I should be going," she said.

I nodded, unable to speak.

"Grammy lives at Number 45," she told me. "Tell your mom that I can stay with you since you can't go to the pool any more. I'll come over here and we'll hang out. If you want."

"She doesn't have a lot of money," I blurted. "I don't know if she can pay much."

Ellis shrugged. "Don't worry about that," she said. "I saved your life, so I guess I'm responsible for you now. Besides, I've got nothing else to do for the rest of the summer."

16

Present day

"**M**ike shouldn't have thrown you out of the pool. I think that was a little extreme," my ten-year-old son observes after I tell him the story of what happened to me at the pool in August of 1969. I smile when Will makes judgments like this, hearing echoes of my kid self, all the outraged chagrin against the injustices of the world.

"The world wasn't as kind back then, Will," I say. "When you screwed up, nobody made excuses for you. Nobody patted your head and told you it was all right, when it wasn't. I'm sure Mike was just imagining his name in all the headlines: Head Guard of Public Pool Lets Ten-Year-Old Drown Under His Nose. Mike must have been furious with me. And he had every right to be."

Lately, Will's been asking me a lot about stuff I remember from my childhood. He's at that age where he's starting to think about his history; it helps to ground him. His mother doesn't care for rehashing and reflecting—she's more of a doer than a thinker. So, Will seeks me out on those occasions when he wants to look backwards. He sprawls long-legged in the nearest chair and asks his questions.

Will is the youngest of our kids—the unexpected third, conceived when his mother was well over forty. The pregnancy set us on our heels at first. The twins were just starting high school when the plus sign appeared on the little pink stick. We had sat on the edge of the bed with the breath knocked out of us. Then my wife stood up and went into the guest room with a tape measure and a spiral notebook and started making plans for a nursery.

It's funny how details I haven't thought of in years come rising so quickly to the surface when Will tests the waters of my memory. Even my mother, who I see quite often, comes back to me precisely the way she was that summer. Her short white hair evaporates, the wrinkles disappear, the wide smile recedes and tightens, and she is that young woman in the loose blonde ponytail, wearing her mustard-coloured waitress dress while she stands slouched over at the kitchen sink, washing the supper dishes.

My mother was always tired back then. It's hard to predict the responses of people when they are perpetually exhausted, especially when you are only ten years old. With my mother, I had to throw things out without having any idea of where they would land. I held my breath a lot in those days.

August, 1969

A few minutes after Ellis left the day we met for the first time, I heard the key in the door. Since day camp ended shortly before my mother got off the bus, she allowed me to walk home and let myself into the apartment. I was only on my own for ten minutes, and I wasn't supposed to tell anyone. I was expected to wash my hands and set the table for supper. Every morning, Mom reminded me that I was not to touch the stove. I would roll my eyes when she administered this serious, yet ludicrous, instruction. What on earth would I want to touch the stove for? I was a ten-year-old boy and I didn't know how to boil an egg. Nor did

I have any interest in doing so, even if I'd possessed the know-how.

I had laid the cloth, set out two mismatched plates, forks and knives, and two cloudy plastic glasses. The bread and butter and ketchup were in their customary spots in the centre of the table. My transistor radio sat on the counter top, crackling out "Love Child" by Diana Ross and the Supremes. I sang along despondently as I flung paper napkins down next to the plates. Some kid at the diner where my mother worked had left the radio behind, and it had sat unclaimed under the cash register for months. Finally, Cookie said to Mom, "I'm tired of looking at this thing day after day. Take it home for your kid." It was my prized possession, even though Mom had warned me that if someone did come looking for it, I'd have to do the right thing and surrender it. I lived in a constant, low-grade fever of anxiety, worrying that I'd have to give the radio up.

Cookie was the owner of the diner, my mother's boss. He'd bought the diner right before he got married, and then brought his new bride to live above the establishment. He and his wife ran the place for almost forty years. When his wife died suddenly of a heart attack (out back, during a bread delivery), Cookie closed the diner for three days and was back at it the day after the funeral. He hired a few waitresses— one full-time to help with breakfast and lunch (my mother), and a couple of high-school girls to help over supper and on Saturdays. His feet were bad, forcing him to limp and hobble behind the counter. Around his ears spurted tufts of wiry grey hair, but above them, his head was completely bald, shining with sweat and a thin layer of grease from hours bent over the grill. Cookie was not a cheerful man. He worked six days a week with no holidays, and he was lonely. Still, although he came off as cranky, Cookie had a good heart, no matter how hard he tried to hide it.

Mom came into the kitchen, carrying a brown paper bag. She was still wearing her apron over her mustard-yellow waitress dress. It was covered in gravy smears and grease spots. Her ponytail had loosened. Pale tendrils of escaped hair fell over her eyes. She would have been around twenty-seven years old then. To my ten-year-old self, she did not seem that young. My mother was beautiful, but I didn't notice very often. In the evenings, when I saw her, she was spent and tired and disheveled. She was kind but sharp; loving but not demonstrative. I loved her fiercely, although we butted heads often.

"Hi, Mom."

"Hi, Davy. Oh, God. My feet. I brought meatloaf and mashed potatoes. And half a pie." She sank into a chair and studied me with her dark eyes.

"What kind?" I asked, trying to avoid her gaze.

"Coconut cream, you'll be glad to know," she replied. "Turn that radio off, will you? I've had enough noise today."

I went to the counter and twisted the dial. Diana Ross and the Supremes disappeared in a final blip of static.

Mom continued to look at me with narrowed eyes. "What's wrong?"

Mom had that unnerving skill bestowed upon mothers the world over who know immediately when something is off-kilter in the universes of their progeny.

"I can't go back to the pool for the rest of the summer." There was no point in hedging. It would just make things worse.

Mom tossed the paper bag onto the table. "What on earth did you do to get thrown out of the pool? Look me in the eye."

I sat across from her and folded my hands on the

table.

"Truth," she warned.

"I snuck into the deep end."

"Why would you do that?"

"To practice," I whispered. "Without everybody staring at me."

"The lifeguards get paid to stare at you," Mom said. "So you won't drown."

I swallowed. "I almost did drown. This girl pulled me out. And then Mike said I couldn't come back for the rest of the summer."

"What do you mean, you almost drowned?"

"I sank to the bottom."

"Davy!"

"I'm all right."

"Thanks to that lifeguard who saw you!"

"It wasn't a lifeguard; it was just a girl. A kid."

Mom leaned back in her hair, shaking her head. "Do you realize what could have...I mean, Davy. Do you have any idea...?"

"I'm sorry, Mom." My voice quivered.

"Crying isn't going to fix anything." My mother had no patience for tears. She wanted things dealt with and done. No fuss, no mess. I stared fixedly at my plate, blinking the tears back.

"Well," she finally said. "The main thing is, you're all right. But here's the problem. I have to work. I have to put food on this table and pay the rent. I don't ask anything of you except that you behave yourself and stay out of trouble. Well, that hasn't happened, has it?"

"No, Mom."

"The fact remains that I have nowhere to send you tomorrow, and you're too young to stay on your own."

"Ellis will come and stay with me."

"Who," my mother interjected, "is Alice?"

"Ellis," I corrected her. "Ellis, with a short e."

21

"What kind of name is that for a girl? All right, then. Who is this Ellis?"

"She's the girl who pulled me out of the deep end. She saved me. And now, she's responsible for me."

My mother smiled suddenly, but quickly lifted her hand and laid it over her mouth.

"And this Ellis, how old is she?" she said, after recovering her stern demeanour.

"Thirteen."

"That's pretty young," my mother said dubiously. "And besides, I don't have any spare cash to pay for a babysitter. You can bet that pool won't refund me for the two weeks you're not there."

"Ellis doesn't want money," I answered. "She just wants something to do for the rest of the summer. I know where she lives. You could go talk to her."

Mom opened the paper bag and lifted out foil-wrapped packages. "I suppose there isn't much of a choice, is there? You've painted us into a corner here. This is what comes of breaking the rules. You've been a very lucky boy today."

I nodded dejectedly.

"All right, don't look so grim. We'll go see this Ellis girl after supper. Let's have some of this meatloaf. It doesn't appeal to me after serving it all day, but Cookie gave me extra gravy and stuck the pie in the bag. Special for you," she added, giving me a pointed look. I knew she implied that I didn't deserve a gift of this magnitude after my behaviour today.

"Can I have a piece of it?" I dared. "Since Cookie said it was for me?"

No desert for rule-breakers. That was one of my mother's consequences for misbehaviour.

My mother speared a piece of meatloaf and dropped it onto my plate. "I suppose, just this one time," she conceded, after watching me squirm for a bit. "A very small piece. To celebrate the fact that you are still alive to enjoy this gourmet fare with me. Let's toast to it. Where's the Freshie?"

I leapt from my chair and yanked on the fridge handle. "I forgot to put it out."

"What colour did you make? I hope it's red."

"It's orange," I said, putting the plastic pitcher on the table.

"Oh, orange," Mom said, regretfully. "Never mind. Fill her up." She pushed her plastic cup towards me and sighed.

My first post-near-death meal. Meatloaf and mashed potatoes and coconut cream pie never tasted so good. We picked up our cups and toasted my good fortune with the disappointing orange Freshie.

"To being alive," my mother said as we raised our red plastic cups.

"I'll drink to that," I said, and swallowed it all down in two gulps. I stifled a belch. "Mom, what's a love child?"

Mom closed her eyes and sat back in her chair. "Davy."

"What? I want to know."

"Yes, I can see that," Mom sighed. "All right, then. It's a baby that's born when its parents aren't married."

"Oh," I said. "Am I a love child?"

"Davy," she sighed again.

"Well, I don't have a dad. Were you married to my dad?"

"No, Davy."

"Did he see me when I was a baby?"

Mom stood and took her dirty plate to the sink. "I'll tell you about that some other time."

"Mom, you always say that."

"Don't argue with me."

"But..."

"Davy!" Mom turned to face me with her hands

jammed on her hips. "Haven't you had enough trouble for one day? You're in no position to make demands of me. Now clear up your dishes and don't say another word about this right now."

She turned back to the sink and twisted the taps. Hot water gushed, the fridge groaned. I took my dirty plate to the counter and slipped away into my room.

I lay on my bed, staring up at the ceiling, twiddling the edge of Boo's worn-thin ear with my thumb. I'd been through all my mother's drawers, looking for some hint of my father, and it wasn't easy to find opportunities to search. I usually did it when she went into the bathroom and ran water for a bath, or if she dozed off in front of the television set. I was pretty much in a sweat every time I slid a drawer open, thinking she would come in and catch me. The topic of my father was obviously a contentious one; I recognized this from an early age. My mother was not someone I cared to rankle, but my curiosity burned. I'd struggled through the dim corridors of my memory over and over again, searching for scraps and shadows, but there was nothing there. Not a single image or word.

Was my father dead? Was he a criminal? Was he in jail?

In the sixties, most kids had fathers and houses with yards and family cars and mothers to greet them at the door when they came home from school. That previous spring, I was the only kid in my class who didn't have a dad to make a Father's Day card for. The other kids had sat, hunched and intent over their desks, crayoning stick figures with fishing poles or golf clubs, earnestly copying a little verse from the black board about hard-working fathers. When I'd approached my teacher at her desk, she had hurriedly whispered to just make a card for a special person in my life. So, I'd drawn Cookie, standing with his bald head and spatula in front of his grill, and written, "YOU MAKE GOOD FRIES." I ripped the card up on my way home, even though it looked a lot like Cookie and had more dimension than the sticks with heads that the other kids had drawn. Maybe I should have given it to him. Cookie and his wife had never had children. He might have liked to tape it to his fridge upstairs in his lonely apartment above the diner. Making good fries didn't seem like enough to commend, and I had been too distraught and self-conscious at the moment to think of anything better.

In spite of many furtive attempts, my mother's drawers and shelves remained empty of any clues about the man who had been my father. There wasn't a note, nor an old photograph, no old diaries or letters. I knew very little at the age of ten about reproductive mysteries, but I had the wherewithal to know that if all the other kids had fathers, then I must, too. Mom had not denied this fact, just expressed emphatically her unwillingness to talk about it. I didn't even have relatives to ask. Mom had been an only child, and her parents did not communicate with her. I'd asked if they were still alive, and her reply had been, "As far as I know. They weren't nice people, Davy, and I don't want you to trouble yourself about them."

I guessed that the man who had been my father must look something like me. I didn't have my mother's pale, straight hair, nor her dark eyes. My hair was thick and shaggy, and my eyes were blue. Other children resembled one parent or the other and I looked nothing like my mother. Still, I knew better than to ask her about it. My mother had clearly defined limits to her patience. Since it was me who was most often the source of the testing of those limits, I knew when to back off.

Nevertheless, it irked me that my mother would keep even the most basic information from me. Did I not have the right to know my father's name? Maybe he'd been looking for me all my life. Maybe my mother had kept me hidden to punish him for something. Maybe he was a decent guy. Maybe he flew airplanes or played the drums in a band. Maybe he owned a circus. Maybe he was a famous artist, or a doctor working on a cure for some horrible disease.

I buried my face in my pillow and swore. The Maybe Game could go on for hours. I'd played it so many times. I knew that as long as my father was a nameless shadow, there was no point in continuing to indulge in it, yet my imagination kept yanking doors open in spite of my resistance.

The corridor in my mind was lined with men, standing quietly for my inspection—cowboys and hippies and soldiers, firemen and farmers and movie stars, all of them tall and sandy-haired. All of them insisting that they were the one.

Present day

In Will's class at school, there are more kids without fathers than there are with fathers. Things have changed radically since 1969, the definition of family being at the top of the list. I know from experience that fractured families are not ideal. But the tendency to ostracize children who live in these circumstances through no fault of their own is one aspect of the "good old days" that I don't miss. It fills me with sad amazement to think that bullying of this nature was not uncommon in our society as recently as forty years ago.

It wasn't that people threw stones at me wherever I went or hurtled epithets such as "Bastard!" at me as I walked down the street—nothing as obvious as that. However, being ignored and disregarded were every bit as painful as any outward show of distaste, and this is what many parents encouraged their children to do. "Don't be mean to Davy," those apron-clad, cookie-making mothers must have instructed their children, as they buttoned their coats to their chins and passed them their lunch boxes in the morning before sending them off to school. "Just don't get too close to him." All through my early years of school, I was not invited to a single birthday party. As for my own birthdays, my mother didn't have the money to throw parties, and even if she had, there was no one from my class at school who would have come. As

I never knew anything else, I grew up accepting of my situation and found bits of happiness in my own lonely corners.

When I was eleven, my mother got married and we moved away. Being in a new school with a new name was the equivalent of a figurative giant eraser. No one knew anything about my past. Once I realized how radically a ten-minute ceremony could change everything for me, I embraced a new life where I was included. There were soccer matches and baseball games at recess, desserts to trade at lunch, kids shouting out my name during name-picks in gym class. I was a boy of many faults—impulsive and quick to anger—but once I found my new place, I resolved to include "invisible" kids in the things I was doing. Sometimes, that involved fists and detentions and lines after school and calls home. Not everyone agreed with my convictions. And often, when it came to teachers and administrators, rules were more important than the bigger picture.

After the wedding, my mother, her husband, and I moved into a house with a big back yard and a basement rec room. I was encouraged to have friends over. My new dad signed me up for baseball and hockey and never missed a game. When he wasn't cheering, he was coaching. Most nights, after supper, Dad would take me out in the yard or out to the road and we would kick a ball around, or whip snowballs, or play catch, and talk about things. Even when the girls came along, he always found time for me. I could tell that he didn't want me to feel replaced by his "real" kids. I can't recall an incident where I was ever treated as anyone other than his son. Mom's husband adopted me as soon as I agreed to it—and that didn't take long.

As I continued to grow up, Dad often acted as a buffer between my mother and me. As close as our previous circumstances had made us, Mom and I were like oil and water. Dad understood both of us so well; he was the perfect neutralizer when things got toxic.

As a grandfather, Dad is just as great. Will and his older brothers, Cooper and Sam, could not have a more wonderful Grampy than my Dad.

August, 1969

After supper on the day I was evicted from the public pool, once the plates and cups were put away, the sink and taps shined up, the tablecloth shaken of its crumbs, and the orange moustache scrubbed off my upper lip, Mom and I put our shoes on and went up the basement stairs. I'd slipped the transistor radio into my pocket, but Mom had noticed the square-shaped bulge and told me to leave the radio at home. I'd known enough to obey immediately and put it on my desk, but my teeth were on edge.

"Why doesn't Mr. Mosely clean up the yard?" I grumbled as Mom locked the door. "I wish I could play back there."

"Use of the yard is not included in the rent."

"Mr. Mosely never uses it," I argued. "And he doesn't even have a job. He has time to do some work back there."

"The park is just down the street."

"But I wish I could play here."

"If wishes were horses," my mother said. It was one of her customary responses to complaints, and it never failed to exasperate me. And it also signaled the conclusion of a discussion. End of subject.

We headed down the sidewalk towards Number 45. The street was filled with kids on bikes and girls skipping at the ends of their driveways. At that period in my life, I sometimes found my hand of its own accord reaching for my mother's whenever we walked somewhere together. It was one of the last remnants of my early childhood resurfacing. I stuffed my hands into the pockets of my shorts to prevent this catastrophe from happening in front of witnesses.

My mother didn't realize it, but I knew the truth about Mr. Mosely. He was a weirdo. He didn't have a job. He hardly ever came out of his house (which had been left to him by his mother). I was privy to these details because I'd overheard my mother talking about Mr. Mosely one night with one of her friends while they were sitting at the kitchen table and I was supposed to be sleeping. We very rarely saw Mr. Mosely at our door—my mother was fastidious about getting the rent check into his mailbox on time. But a few months back, he'd knocked when my mother was in the bath, and I went up and opened the door. He stood there, trembling.

"H...Hello," he stammered. "Is your m-mother at home?

"She can't come to the door right now," I said. Mr. Mosely's shirt was buttoned wrong, and he was wearing his house slippers outdoors.

Mr. Mosely peered down at me tremulously from behind his spectacles, with his arms folded tight across his chest as though he were hugging himself. He was quite tall and overly thin. His brown eyes were kind, although timid, and he had a head of unruly dark curls. If he'd just brush his hair and button his shirt right, he wouldn't look like that much of a weirdo, I'd thought.

"W...will you tell your mother that s-someone will be coming to-tomorrow to f-fix the b-bathroom s-sink?"

"Sure, I'll tell her."

"Thanks."

Mr. Mosely's living room must have been right above my bedroom. As I was a chronically poor sleeper as a child, I often heard Mr. Mosely above my head, pacing through the long hours of the night. Sometimes, I heard him weeping up there, through the floorboards. The sound of a man crying was strange and disconcerting to me. I lay in my bed with Boo against my cheek, listening to Mr. Mosely weeping above me. His sobs were long, monotone hums. They would hang, then crash and break, and then the next one would start up again, one after another, like waves at the beach. Groggy with half-sleep, I drifted on the crest of Mr. Mosely's rhythmic sobs, then the refrigerator would drag me beneath the surface with its nightshift clanking and vibrating. The night would pass this way. At breakfast, my mother would remark on the circles under my eyes and wonder how I could be in bed for ten hours and still look like a fifty-year-old insomniac in the morning.

"Here it is. Number 45. My God, what a nicely-kept place," my mother remarked as we turned up the sidewalk and headed towards the front door.

She was right. The house was a massive yellow-brick residence with a wrap-around porch. The trim and shutters were painted dark green. In the front yard were two spreading maples, one of them sporting a tire swing on a long rope. I gave it a wistful look as we walked past.

Mom and I went up the steps onto the porch. There were wicker chairs and rockers, all with plump cushions and pillows. I had a sudden and overwhelming urge to find a book and curl up in one of those chairs. Mom rapped her knuckles on the wide screen door.

An older lady wearing a frilly apron appeared at the end of the long hall inside and came to the door.

"Can I help you?" she said while wiping her floury

hands on her apron. She was tall, like Ellis, and had the same solemn grey eyes. But her dark hair was short and streaked with white.

"I'm Violet Borowski and this is my son, David. We live up the road. I understand there is a girl named Alice living here?"

Ellis, I corrected mentally. Short e. Outwardly, I thought it best to hold my tongue.

"My grand-daughter, Ellis. Is everything all right?"

"Oh, yes. Ellis. Davy told me. Short e. Everything is more than fine. Ellis saved Davy from drowning at the public pool today."

The lady opened the screen door and came out onto the porch. "Please," she said, "sit down. I'll call Ellis. Would you care for some lemonade? I'm Hannah Greary, by the way." She reached out her hand and my mother shook it. Mrs. Greary shook my hand, too.

"Pardon the flour, David." She smiled down at me.

"Nice to meet you," my mother replied. "Don't go to any trouble, Mrs. Greary."

"It's no trouble, and please, call me Hannah. I'm ready for a cold drink myself. I've just taken the last batch of cookies out of the oven. It's rather hot for baking, but I had a hankering for sugar cookies. Would you like cookies with your lemonade, David?"

"Yes, please," I mumbled.

"I'll be back directly," Hannah said. "Please, sit down and be comfortable."

Hannah went through the screen door and it snapped behind her. Mom and I sank into the cushions of a wicker couch. I sat back and leaned my head against a flowery pillow, but Mom perched on the edge of her seat, primly, with her ankles crossed. She had changed out of her mustard-coloured waitress dress into her red skirt and white blouse, and fixed her hair. The maples were filled with twittering birds. Squirrels bounced across the lawn. An orange cat crept up the steps and twisted languorously around my calves. I dropped my hand to stroke its head. On the far end of the porch, I noticed a large doll house with gables. Strangely, there were no dolls in it, or furniture. On the bottom level stood an ivy plant in a little pot, and the bright green vines and leaves twisted up the staircase, through the little rooms, and out the windows. I walked over to have a closer look.

"Don't touch anything, Davy," my mother warned.

I dropped to my knees in front of the doll house. On closer examination, I saw that it was filled with all kinds of interesting little objects—sparkly stones in the kitchen, beach glass on the bedroom floor, the blue-green shells of robins' eggs in the bathroom, a pile of glossy acorns in the parlour. Rose petals were scattered throughout. Fresh ones.

The screen door opened, and Hannah came out with a tray of glasses and a plate of golden cookies. Ellis followed with a tall glass pitcher brimming with pink lemonade. My mouth watered just thinking of that lemonade. I had milk with my breakfast and Freshie or water all the other times. Lemonade was a rare treat.

"Oh, I see you've found one of Ellis's corners," Hannah remarked to me.

Ellis had changed into a white T-shirt and a pair of cut-off shorts. Her arms were smooth and tanned. She set the pitcher on the table next to my mother. "Hello, Davy."

I smiled shyly and gave her a little wave. Ellis's hair was damp, falling around her shoulders and down her back. The smell of shampoo and soap drifted over and tickled my nostrils.

"I picked some raspberries this morning, and I crushed a few and mixed them in the lemonade," Hannah said, filling the glasses. "Come have a drink, David."

Ellis sat down and took a cookie from the plate. "These are Grammy's specialty," she said, taking a bite. "Try one."

She didn't have to tell me twice. I took a cookie and bit into it—buttery and sweet, still warm and soft from the oven. I sighed with pleasure and reached for a glass of lemonade, flushed pink with crushed raspberries. There were ice cubes in it, and condensation ran down the sides of the glass.

"David's mother tells me there was an incident at the pool today," Hannah said to Ellis.

"Yes," Ellis replied. "Davy sank to the bottom of the deep end. I saw him go down and I pulled him out."

"He would have drowned otherwise," my mother said. "I want to thank you for saving Davy's life, Ellis."

Ellis took a swallow of lemonade. "That's okay," she answered. "I'm glad he's all right."

I caught my mother's eye and then looked pointedly at the plate of cookies. Mom nodded her assent, and I reached for another one.

"Did the lifeguards not see that David was in trouble?" Hannah asked.

"He wasn't supposed to be in the deep end," my mother explained. "He snuck in. And did a good job of remaining unnoticed by the lifeguards. Luckily, your grand-daughter has a sharp eye."

"She does, at that," said Hannah. She and Ellis exchanged kind looks.

My mother gave me a studied glance, and I looked at my feet.

"Davy tells me that Ellis offered to watch him for a few weeks," my mother said. "You see, he's been banned from the pool after his exploits of today and I have no one to mind him while I'm at work. The lady next door watches him after school, but she's not around in the summers. I bought a park and pool

34

pass for the summer, so he had supervised play in the morning and then went to the pool for the afternoon. But now..." she sighed.

Hannah nodded. "Ellis is good with younger children. As you already know, she is a very responsible girl. If Ellis wants the job, I see no reason why she shouldn't do it."

My mother looked uncomfortable. "I won't be able to pay her much," she said. "I'm a waitress, and we get by, but..."

"I already told Davy I don't care about that," Ellis interrupted. "I'm happy to have something to do."

"There you go," said Hannah. "That's all settled then. Ellis is welcome to bring David over here for lunch every day, since you live nearby. They can go back and forth between houses if they want to."

"Really?" my mother exclaimed. "Oh, God—that is so nice of you. Of both of you." She looked at me. "Now, Davy..."

"I'll be good. I promise," I mumbled, humiliated.

"He really is a good boy," my mother told Hannah. "He makes mistakes, but he's a good boy."

"That's easy to see," said Hannah. "Let's say no more about it. What time shall Ellis be over in the morning?"

The sun was setting, hovering at the edge of the sky and casting a warm glow through the trees and across the floor of the porch. While the two women talked, I watched as Ellis stood and walked over to the dollhouse. She sat down in front of it with her legs crossed like a yogi. Her hands reached in, rearranging the sparkling stones and spreading the rose petals. I went to stand beside her.

"What's all this stuff for?" I said. "Where's the furniture?"

Ellis glanced up at me. "I don't play with dolls any more. It's just a pretty spot I made."

"Why?" I said.

"It's just something I do," Ellis said.

I wormed in beside her and reached into the bedroom for a piece of beach glass. It was dark blue, luminous, edges worn smooth by sand and water. I rolled it between my fingers and around my palm. It would have been simple to slip it into my pocket, and although I considered it at great length, in the end, I propped it up in a corner of the doll house bedroom. I didn't want anything to mess up my chances of having Ellis as my babysitter; I'd wreaked enough havoc for one day.

That night, after I'd gone to bed, it was stifling and hot in my room. The small window didn't allow for much air circulation. I tossed and turned under the sheet, flipping my pillow, looking for a spot that would stay cool long enough for me to get to sleep. I was almost there when the sound of Mr. Mosely's ghostly sobbing started. I rolled over onto my back and made a cradle for my head with my arms. The muted crying seeped through the ceiling, making vaporous shapes, like smoke and shadow. I watched Mr. Mosely's misery wander and unfurl along the ceiling tiles.

My fingers fumbled until they found Boo. I set him on my chest, over my heart, for protection—in case the misery got heavy, like rain in clouds, and washed over me.

August, 1969

My mother's shifts at Cookie's started at 7:00 each morning. Earlier in that summer of 1969, when I was going to the park for day camp, Mom would walk with me on her way to the bus stop. Now that Ellis was coming, my mother told me I could stay in bed a little longer if I liked.

However, that first day, I was so excited about Ellis coming that I was out of bed and dressed well before my mother emerged from her room. Mom shuffled into the kitchen, with her hair all rolled in spongy curlers and her pink puffy mules smacking the yellowed linoleum, and regarded me with surprise. I was making toast, popping it up every thirty seconds because the automatic part was busted. If I didn't, the bread would blacken to ashes down inside the toaster while the kitchen filled with smoke. On burnt-toast days, Mom would stomp around the apartment, opening windows and exclaiming bitterly. It was no way to start the day. I commissioned myself toast-watcher.

"Up already? What's all the excitement?" Mom reached for the tea kettle. She would have her coffee at the diner before her shift started, but she always had a cup of tea at home.

"No excitement," I denied, plucking the hot toast out of the slot and tossing it onto a plate. "I'm just hungry."

"Make me a piece," said Mom, as she rifled through the cupboard for a box of teabags.

I dug the knife into the peanut butter and slathered it across the toast, then plopped on a spoonful of jam. "You can have this one," I said, and dropped another piece of bread into the toaster. "Mom, why can't we get a new toaster?"

"The one we have works perfectly well." Mom took her toast to the table and lowering herself into a chair. "Why waste money on a new toaster when we already have one that does the job?"

"It does a pretty piss-poor job, if you ask me."

"Davy," my mother admonished. "I don't like that schoolyard talk. I hope you won't speak that way when Ellis is here."

"Sorry."

There was a knock at the door above us.

"She's early," my mother said while picking up her plate. "Let Ellis in while I get dressed."

Ellis stood at the door, with her long dark hair caught in a high ponytail. She regarded me with her serious grey eyes. In her hands, she held a large bouquet of wet yellow flowers.

"Hi, Davy."

"Hi," I said. "Come on in. Want some toast? Toast!" I shouted and plunged down the stairs. I popped the bread up before the smoke started, but the toast was too black to eat. I quickly stuffed it into the garbage can. "That was close," I said. Ellis looked around the little kitchen.

"Yes, please. I would like some toast. Do you have a jar for these flowers? Grammy let me pick them from her garden. I thought your mom might like them for the table."

"Yeah, I think my mom has some old jars under here." I dropped to the floor and scavenged under the sink. "How's this one?" I lifted a dusty old pickle jar for her inspection.

"Fine," said Ellis. "Can you rinse it out and put some water in it?"

When Mom came into the kitchen, Ellis and I were sitting at the table with our toast, and the yellow flowers were in the centre.

"Black-Eyed Susans," Mom said. "They're so pretty." She reached out and stroked the deep yellow petals. "They're still wet from the dew."

"I cut them first thing this morning," Ellis said.

"They make the kitchen look nicer."

It was true. Some of the dinginess seemed to have evaporated from the kitchen. I looked at the flowers, sitting in a circle of sunlight, and munched my toast.

"I have to get going," Mom said. She gave her hair a pat. "Ellis, I put the emergency numbers near the phone in the living room. Help yourself to whatever is in the fridge. I'll be home around 4:30. Davy, make sure you set the table. And don't touch the stove."

"I won't," I sighed.

"You need a haircut," she said, tousling my sandy locks on her way past. "We'll do it before school starts. Bye, kids," she said, and she rushed up the stairs.

I groaned. "Not a haircut."

Ellis raised her eyebrows. "What's wrong with getting a haircut?"

"Nothing, if Mom would take me to a barber. She cuts my hair herself. And she does a piss...I mean, she doesn't do a very good job."

"Grammy was a hairdresser when she was younger. Maybe she could cut your hair."

"Like, she cut girls' hair?" I said, skeptically.

"She cut everyone's hair. She used to cut soldiers' hair during the war. Buzzed it right off."

"I don't want to be bald. Mom's boss, Cookie, is bald. You can almost see your reflection in his head."

"Grammy wouldn't make you bald unless you

wanted to be. Now, I was thinking we could do something in your backyard today."

I perked up. "But it might be dangerous back there. Broken glass and stuff. And I don't know if Mr. Mosely would like it."

"We'll just find a little corner and fix it up a bit. He won't care if we use one little corner."

"Yeah, he hardly ever comes out anyway," I noted, finding myself quite intrigued with Ellis's idea. I recalled what Hannah had said, when she saw me looking at the dollhouse on her porch the night before. Something about one of Ellis's corners.

"What will we do to the corner?"

"Clean it up a little. Make it look nice. You could go back there and draw, or read. Everyone needs an outside reading spot. It's important. We should do it before it gets too hot."

Ellis and I put our plates in the sink and went outside into the backyard.

"Which corner?" I said, doubtfully. Now that we were out there in the gloomy overgrown wilderness, even a corner seemed a formidable task.

Ellis pointed. "That one behind the shed. There's some sun back there. And no one will see us. Grab one of those garbage cans."

We busied ourselves behind the shed, tossing cans and sticks and heaps of dead leaves into the trash can. Before long, we could see grass beneath our feet. Ellis followed the fence line, tugging weeds.

"That's a lilac bush." Ellis pointed at a tall bush in the corner right behind the shed. "If we clear the dead branches out around the bottom, it'll make a great fort. There should be room at the bottom for you to fit in."

"A fort," I breathed. I had wanted a fort for as long as I could remember.

"Yep," Ellis said. "Let's get to work."

The dead branches snapped off easily, and we tossed them into the can. Soon, there was a little hollow in the centre of the bush that we could squeeze into.

"No one will ever see you in here," Ellis said. The shadows of the lilac leaves dappled across her face and made her grey eyes deepen. My head was almost up to her shoulder. Our sides touched. All the hairs on my arms stood up.

"Let's go to Grammy's and have lunch," Ellis said after a few minutes of a very satisfactory silence. "Tomorrow, we'll paint that old wooden chair under the willow tree. You'll need a place to sit back here when you're drawing."

"I don't have any paint, though."

"Grammy has lots in her tool shed. We'll ask her at lunch."

The sun was high. Sweat ran in my eyes, and I had a raging thirst. In spite of these discomforts, I couldn't remember a more interesting or quickly-passing morning. I locked the apartment door, put the key back under the pot, and Ellis and I headed down the road to Hannah's.

We ran past the tire swing and up the porch steps. Hannah was there, sitting in one of the wicker chairs. "There you are," she said. "I've got your lunch all ready. Go on in and have something to eat. But wash up first," she called after us. "The two of you are filthy!"

The foyer of Hannah's house was as big as our living room. I stood, gawking at the wide staircase with its shimmering stained glass window at the landing, the rich wine-coloured carpet going up the stairs. The large mirror on the wall in front of me reflected that Hannah was right—there was dirt smeared across my face, and my hands were grey with dried mud.

Ellis led me up the long staircase to the bathroom.

There was enough room in that bathroom for thirty people. Our bathroom in the apartment was tiny, the toilet jammed up to the sink, and the tub crowded behind the door. At the gleaming white pedestal sink, I used so much soap that the lather crept up to my elbows. When I dried off on the fluffy white towel, I didn't leave any dirt behind.

I waited in the hall while Ellis washed her hands. All the bedroom doors were open, except for one. I crept along the hallway, peeking inside every one of them. The one at the end of the hall was Hannah's—I saw the dress she'd been wearing the night before draped over a chair, and the room smelled of scented talcum powder. One of the dresser drawers was slightly open, and the night stand was cluttered with a stack of books, some pill bottles, a pair of glasses, and a half-filled glass of water. The other rooms were tidy, but unoccupied. The beds were perfectly made, the curtains closed, and the dresser surfaces bare.

That left the room with the closed door. The water in the bathroom was still running. I inched over to the door and quietly turned the handle. This must be Ellis's room, I thought. I was overcome with curiosity. The door silently glided open a crack, and I moved my head closer to peer inside.

"Davy," said Ellis. I almost jumped out of my skin.

"What?" I squeaked.

"Don't go in there, all right?"

"I wasn't going to...I was just..." I stammered. Ellis had her arms folded across her chest as she looked at me. Her eyebrows were slightly drawn together; she looked disapproving.

"Is this your room?" I asked.

"That's where I sleep, yes. I'm sorry, Davy. I'm not angry with you. I just don't like it when anyone goes in there. OK?"

"OK," I answered.

"Thanks. Let's go down for lunch."

Hannah was in the kitchen when we entered. There were three plates set at the table. Another bouquet of Black-Eyed Susans sat in the middle next to a basket of crusty rolls. There was a plate with thick slabs of ham and slices of cheese, a bowl filled with carrot and celery sticks, and a glass dish of pickles. Hannah filled three glasses with lemonade. Raspberries bobbed at the top.

"It's just sandwiches today," Hannah said, as though the feast in front of us was nothing special. I took the same lunch to school or to day camp every day—a flattened peanut butter sandwich with jam leaking through the bread, a thermos of Freshie, and maybe an apple or an orange, if we had any. My stomach almost turned upside down with its sudden, violent rumbling.

Hannah gestured to a chair. "Sit and eat. Looks like the two of you had a busy morning. Worked up an appetite, did you?"

Nodding, I slid into a chair and took a roll out of the basket that Ellis passed me.

"These are Grammy's homemade rolls," Ellis said. "She made the pickles, too."

"Old family recipe," Hannah said, buttering her roll. "These pickles are last year's. I haven't done pickles this summer. It's been busy with Ellis here."

Ellis stacked ham and cheese onto her bun, picked it up, and took a bite. My mouth watered and I set to work making my sandwich. Hannah put some carrot sticks on my plate.

"So, what were you two up to this morning?" Hannah said, and took a sip of lemonade.

"We're making a spot in Davy's back yard where he can read and draw," Ellis explained. "We also made a fort."

Hannah smiled. "Could this be another one of

Ellis's corners developing?"

Corners again. I would have asked about it, but my mouth was stuffed with cheese and pickles.

"Can I take some paint and brushes tomorrow to paint a chair for Davy's corner?" Ellis said.

"Sure. Just clean the brush when you're done and make sure everything goes back where you found it. What are you planning for the afternoon?"

"Can Davy play here?"

"If he wants to. Maybe the two of you could pick a row of beans for me?"

"Sure," I said. "I'll pick beans. So long as I don't have to eat them."

Hannah laughed. "Well, I won't force you."

After lunch, Ellis pushed me in the tire swing while her grandmother went upstairs for a rest.

"Do you stay here every summer?" I called out on a downswing. I sailed back up, towards the lower limbs of the maple, reveling in the feeling of being airborne.

"Yes," Ellis said. "Usually for two weeks. Never for the whole summer like this time."

"Why are you here for the whole summer then?" I craned my head around to look at her.

"One more big push," Ellis said, "and then it's time to pick the beans."

I'd learned from interactions with my mother when to push for information and when to shut up. I leapt from the swing and followed Ellis.

There was an enormous garden at the back of the house: onions with their leggy sprouts drooping to the ground, carrots with their feathery tops, beets with leaves veined in purple, cucumber vines winding over the ground, delicate fronds of dill, and several long rows of green beans. Ellis told me the names of everything as we walked through the rows.

"Doesn't your grandmother live by herself?"

"Yes, most of the time."

"How does she eat all this stuff?"

"Oh, she freezes it or cans it, and then she shares it with people."

Ellis passed me a pail and we bent to pick the beans. When we brought the pails into the kitchen later, Hannah had a cold drink and sugar cookies for us.

"Why don't you two sit out on the porch for a bit and cool off?" Hannah suggested. "Then you'd better head to David's. It's going on four o'clock."

"Already?" I exclaimed.

"Have you had a good day, David?" Hannah smiled.

I nodded, trying to be nonchalant. "Yeah. It was fine."

My day had been more than good, but I knew it would seem pathetic to these people. A swing and a sandwich and an old lilac bush. It wouldn't seem like much to them. To me, it added up to the best day of my entire life.

August, 1969

The next three days dissolved in a flurry of busyness. We worked on the back yard corner in the mornings, and then spent the afternoon at Hannah's house. After a wonderful lunch (which I would devour like a farm labourer), we put some time in the garden and then fell into porch chairs with a stack of old Archie comics. We took turns pushing one another in the tire swing, and before I knew it, it was time for Ellis to walk me back home.

One morning, Ellis brought over two brushes and a can of deep blue exterior paint, and we took the old chair that was on its side under the willow behind the shed to paint it. The next day, when it was dry, I took a little jar of leftover gold model paint from my desk and Ellis and I painted stars and moons all over it. We took some of the old terracotta pots that were piled up at the side of the house and filled them with dirt. Hannah had an enormous geranium bed at the side of her house—pink, white and red ones, and she let Ellis and I dig a few of them out. My corner had a little row of potted geraniums against the fence which I watered every morning, filling a pail in the apartment sink and dragging it up the stairs and outside. I put my chair under the shade of the lilac bush. Ellis christened it the Starry Night Chair after Vincent Van Gogh's painting, which, at the time, I had never heard of.

One morning, we took a breather from our work. I was sitting inside the lilac bush fort, and Ellis was perched on the Starry Night Chair. A cardinal sent out a piercing call from the top of the shed. Cicadas sawed through the hot air with their harsh, end-of-summer drone.

"Were you really serious when you said you didn't have any friends, Davy?" Ellis suddenly said.

"Yeah," I replied, from the centre of the lilac bush. "Nobody really seems to like me."

"Are the other kids mean to you?"

"Well, no. They aren't mean, really. They just don't talk to me. It's like they don't see me, like I'm invisible."

I thought ahead to the first day of school, which was rapidly approaching. I would walk into the school yard, where all the kids yell and tear around. I'd find my customary spot against the wall and stand there watching, like I always did. Boys would run by, and I would give them a quick smile, but they wouldn't notice. Maybe a soccer ball would roll my way, and I'd kick it back in the direction it had come from. There might be a distant "thanks," but it wasn't really directed at me in particular.

At noon, I'd go into the lunch room and take out my jam-soggy sandwich and eat it in silence. The other kids would chat quietly, sharing their Twinkies and their potato chips. On the television perched atop the tall stand at the front of the room, the Road Runner's tongue would dart out and the Coyote would inevitably fall off another cliff. I would keep my eyes fixed on the screen, pretending to watch, trying not to appear pitiful. I would sit in my little square of silence and wait for someone to join me, and no-one ever would. No one ever had. Until Ellis.

"It's probably because I don't have a dad," I finally said.

There was a long silence. Finally, Ellis whispered, "You're not invisible, Davy. And I like you."

Inside the lilac bush, where she couldn't see me, a smile spread over my face. I got to all fours and peered out from underneath the bush. I saw Ellis's flip-flops on the ground and her bare toes wiggling in the grass. They had dark pink nail polish on them.

Then I saw another pair of feet. Big ones, clad in house slippers.

"W-what is g-going on b-back here?" said a trembling, low voice.

Shit, it was Mr. Mosely. I froze inside the lilac bush.

"I'm minding Davy Barowski," Ellis said, jumping to her feet. "I brought him back here to play."

I found my limbs and tumbled out from under the lilac bushes. "Here I am," I said. Ellis grabbed my hands and helped me to my feet.

Mr. Mosely grasped the top of the chair with his shaking hands. "I saw g-garden re-refuse in the trash can," he said. "W-what are you d-doing?" Behind his glasses, his eyes were wide, and his jaw was working. His face was red and perspiring.

"We just cleaned up a corner so Davy can play back here," Ellis said. "I hope it's all right."

Mr. Mosely's eyes took in the chair he was leaning on and the potted geraniums and the tidy plot of ground, where all the garbage and sticks and leaves had been cleared. He stared at us. My heart was beating like a trip-hammer. The last thing I needed was to get into more trouble. My mother would go berserk. I edged closer to Ellis.

"W-why did-didn't you a-ask first?" Mr. Mosely demanded.

Ellis laid her arm around my shoulders. "It was my idea. I told Davy you probably wouldn't mind. I'm really sorry."

Mr. Mosely looked down at his hands, still clenching the top of the chair. "Th-this old ch-chair," he said. "I f-forgot about it. M-my m-mother used to r-rest in it after her gar-gardening. You p-painted it?"

"I thought it was thrown away," Ellis explained.

"It l-looks b-beautiful," Mr. Mosely said. "T-this whole cor-corner looks b-beautiful. You've done s-such a nice j-job."

Ellis and I looked at one another in delighted shock, scarcely believing what we'd just heard.

"D-do you think you could f-fix another c-corner for me?" Mr. Mosley asked. "One c-closer to the h-house, maybe?"

"Yes," Ellis and I exclaimed together.

"I h-have to go in now," Mr. Mosely said, with his knuckles white against the Starry Night Chair. I realized then that Mr. Mosely had not been angry at all. He'd been scared. What could Mr. Mosely have to be afraid of back here? Not us, surely? Why would a grown man be afraid of two kids? He turned and almost ran towards the back door.

As he strode quickly through the weeds, Ellis called, "We'll get started tomorrow!"

Mr. Mosely raised his hand briefly and disappeared into the house.

We raced over to Hannah's for lunch and sat chattering about our plans for Mr. Mosely's corner, almost too excited to eat. Hannah had made baked macaroni and cheese with cut-up hotdogs in it, and there were sliced cucumbers and tomatoes from the garden. The kitchen smelled like heaven.

"There's something not right with Mr. Mosely," Ellis said. "He was shaking like a leaf."

"Yeah, he's kind of a weirdo," I replied, shaking ketchup out of the bottle until it splatted all over my macaroni. I clamped my mouth closed and looked at Hannah. Weirdo was probably not the best choice of words, but Hannah didn't say anything, just continued to cut up her tomatoes with her fork and knife.

"It was like he was terrified to be out in the yard," Ellis mused. "He had to hold onto the chair just to keep his knees from knocking together."

"It sounds like he's agoraphobic," Hannah said while pouring iced tea into our glasses.

"Agora-what?" I scooped up a fork of macaroni and shoved it into my mouth.

"Agoraphobic. It's an illness of the mind where people panic every time they try to leave their house."

"Yeah," I mumbled through my mouth full of food. "Mr. Mosely never leaves his house. We hardly ever see him. And he doesn't have a job. He's in there all day and night. Sometimes," I added, "he cries. I can hear him in my room underneath." I felt a little stab of guilt. That last bit had been rather unnecessary. I shouldn't have told that part.

Hannah shook her head. "Poor man. It sounds like one of Ellis's corners will do him some good. That's a nice project for the two of you. Take anything you need from the tool shed and help yourself to whatever you can find up in the attic that might be useful."

"We'll clear away some of the junk in Mr. Mosely's yard tomorrow morning," said Ellis.

That night, I wasn't awake long enough to hear Mr. Mosely up above me, crying through the floorboards. After my bath, I got into bed with my drawing pad to make some plans for the new corner. My radio was on the pillow beside me, and the Temptations were singing "I Wish it Would Rain."

My head had sunk down before the end of the song. I was only vaguely aware of Mom coming in and turning off the radio, tipping me over so that I was on my side, and drawing the sheet up around my shoulders.

I didn't move until morning.

6

Present day

"That would suck," Will says, absently tipping back in the kitchen chair he is sitting in. It's a habit of his—drives his mother crazy. She's told him a thousand times to stop, but he doesn't even realize he's doing it. "Not being able to leave the house. How did this guy get groceries and stuff?"

"He had them delivered," I reply, reaching for the teapot and filling my mug. I recall that every Saturday afternoon, a truck pulled up in the driveway, and a delivery boy carried a cardboard box to Mr. Mosely's door. If I happened to be outside, I would come close and peer into the box, curious what Mr. Mosely would be eating that week. Mr. Mosely's tastes were bland and boring—soup, crackers, eggs, milk, arrowroot cookies. The occasional cut of meat wrapped in pink butcher paper, tied up with twine.

"What if he got sick, or hurt, and had to go to the hospital?" Will says.

"I suppose he tried to deal with it at home," I guess.

"What about haircuts?"

"He cut his own hair, probably."

"What about..."

"Will," I interrupt. "The man didn't leave his house. He figured out ways to make it work. I don't know what else to tell you."

Will's face falls, and I rub my temples. I've

disappointed myself so often with this kid. It's almost as though I've used up my allotted store of patience with the twins and there is nothing left over for this one. You would think that I might be able to scrounge some up somewhere, seeing as I was a kid of incessant questions myself.

"Hey, Will," I say, gently. "There's more to the Mr. Mosely story."

August, 1969

The night before Ellis and I were going to make a corner for Mr. Mosely, I had a dream. It was dark, and I was sitting inside the lilac fort. The leaves of the lilac bushes were undulating softly in the night breezes. I sat hugging my knees and looking up, catching glimpses of the starry sky through the moving leaves. Nearby, I heard the sound of approaching footsteps. Mr. Mosely appeared and stood calmly on the grass, tipping his face up to look at the moon.

"Beautiful evening, isn't it, Davy?" he said, without a trace of a stutter.

"Yes," I replied from inside the lilac bush. "Would you like to go for a walk, Mr. Mosely?"

"Why walk when we could fly?" Mr. Mosely smiled. He drew me out of the bush with both hands, and then tossed me up into the sky. I caught the wind like an untied balloon. Laughing, Mr. Mosely launched himself into the air and joined me. We circled above the willow tree, our faces lit up with moonlight. Mr. Mosely reached forward and tapped my shoulder. "You're it," he yelled and shot off towards the moon, me in hot pursuit.

Mom shook me awake. "Time to get up, Davy."

I sat up, rubbing my eyes. "It's still dark. What time is it?" I could still hear the last echoes of Mr.

Mosely's laughter as he swooped through the air in his house slippers.

"It's almost time for Ellis to get here," she replied. "It's pouring rain outside." Mom was dressed for work, already wearing her rubber rain boots.

My heart sank. "But we're supposed to start work on Mr. Mosely's corner today!" I had told my mother all about our backyard encounter with Mr. Mosely over supper the night before.

"Well, you'll have to postpone it," she said. "It's not fit for ducks out there."

The Temptations had jinxed me. "I Wish it Would Rain" might as well have been a rain dance. I flung Boo to the floor and stormed to the bathroom. "This day is ruined," I shouted and slammed the toilet lid up. "I wish it wasn't raining!"

"If wishes were horses," Mom called back. I could hear her fumbling through the closet for her umbrella.

"Those damned horses," I muttered to myself.

"Daaaaaamn," I whispered again, for good measure.

"Davy," said Mom, as I grumbled my way into the kitchen. "Hannah Greary telephoned last night after you went to sleep. She suggested that she might cut your hair the weekend before school starts. We were chatting and I mentioned that you'll be needing a haircut. She told me that she used to be a hairdresser."

"Why can't the barber do it?" I exclaimed. "Just one time, why can't you just take me to the barber and let me get a normal haircut like all the other boys?"

Mom's face flushed. "The barber costs money, which I do not have. Mrs. Greary has been nice enough..."

"Why is there never enough money?" I interrupted. "I can't play baseball because there isn't enough money! I can't have Twinkies in my lunch because there isn't enough money. We can't get a new toaster because there isn't enough money. I can't go to the damn barber because there isn't enough..."

My head jerked back, and there was a searing heat on my cheek. It took me a long moment to realize that Mom had just walloped me across the face. I was rendered mute with astonishment. I stared at her, not believing what had just happened. She stared back at me with flaming cheeks. Tears leapt into my eyes. My mother had never hit me before. I leaned back on the refrigerator door and put my hands over my eyes. The fridge clunked and hummed, vibrating against my back. I sobbed.

Mom knelt in front of me and tried to move my hands away from my face.

"Oh, God. Davy," she said.

"Don't talk to me," I wept and struggled against her. "Leave me alone. I want to go to my room."

"In a minute," she replied. "But first, I want you to hear what I have to say. The other night, you asked me about your dad."

Mom dropped her hands. Through my wet fingers, I could see her kneeling on the kitchen floor in front of me, her face stricken. My heart slammed in my chest, making it hard to catch my breath.

"I had you when I was seventeen years old, Davy," she began. "My boyfriend didn't stick around when I told him I was going to have a baby. When I called him the next day, his parents told me he'd left town, and to never call there again. When I told my parents I was pregnant, they told me I had to leave the house. So, I quit school, took the money I'd saved up for university working at the bowling alley, and left. I got on a bus by myself and stayed on it for two days. When I got out, I was here in this town. I found this apartment, and after you were born, Cookie gave me the job at the diner. No one else wanted to hire me. It was the only job I could get."

I took my hands away from my face. I could see the top of her head, where her hair was pulled tight into a ponytail.

"Do you think I don't want to give you all those things you just mentioned? Do you think I don't want you to have all the things the other boys have? Because I do, Davy. I wish you could have everything."

I hung my head. "If wishes were horses," I whispered.

"Oh, Davy..." Mom struggled for words. "Maybe it's not much," she continued, after she found her voice again. "But what we have here is all I am able to give you. I didn't want to give you up. Maybe that was selfish. But I'm your mother, and I wanted to keep you. I love you."

I climbed down onto the floor and wrapped my arms around her neck. She put her arms around me and tipped her forehead onto the top of my head.

"Your father didn't want us," she said. "But I wanted us. I thought that would be enough."

"It's enough," I wept into her neck. "I'm sorry, Mom."

She squeezed me against her. "I'm sorry, too. I shouldn't have slapped you. That was wrong."

There was a soft tap at the door upstairs. Mom stood. "There's Ellis," she said. "I'll let her in, and then I need to run and catch my bus. Go and wash your face before Ellis comes down. See you tonight. And Davy?"

"What?" I snuffled.

"Don't touch the stove."

I went into the bathroom and beheld my splotched, red face in the mirror. The slapped cheek was vivid and bright. I turned on the cold water. How could I face Ellis looking like this? I filled the sink, sank my face into it, and opened my swollen eyes so the water could bathe them.

My father had taken off when he'd found out about me. There was no doctor or painter or drummer out there, looking for a lost son. I was like the unwanted morsels on a plate, scraped off into the garbage. A smeared page torn out of a book. Disposed of, and forgotten. In the corridor of my mind, all the sandy-haired men I'd ever envisioned slipped through doorways and never looked back. It was so empty in there; it echoed.

"Davy?" Ellis called from the kitchen.

"Be out in a minute!" I sat on the toilet seat, toweling off my wet face. I looked in the mirror again. There wasn't much of an improvement, but I couldn't stay in the bathroom all day. I sighed, and went out to the kitchen.

"Grammy made cinnamon buns," Ellis said, laying plates on the table. "She figured we would be disappointed about the rain, and she says the smell of cinnamon is good medicine for disappointments. She sent some over for Mr. Mosely, so I knocked at his door a minute ago and delivered them. I told him we'd start on the corner next week...what's wrong?"

I slid into my chair. "Mom and I had an argument. It's all right now."

Ellis gave me a steady look. "Oh," she finally said.

"Do you ever have arguments with your mom?" I said.

Ellis blinked and looked away. I realized then that I hadn't heard anything about Ellis's parents since I'd met her. I didn't even know if she had siblings. Or where she lived when she wasn't at her grandmother's.

"We used to," she finally said. She lifted a sheet of waxed paper and took two cinnamon buns off a plate. "Let's have breakfast," she said. "And then we'll find a corner in here to fix up. All right?"

"Here? Like in the apartment, you mean?"

"Yes."

My spirits lifted a little.

"And this afternoon," Ellis continued, "We'll go up to Grammy's attic and find some stuff to use for Mr. Mosely's corner."

After we'd eaten Hannah's cinnamon rolls and licked the icing off our fingertips, we went around the apartment looking for a corner to brighten.

"What's in there?" asked Ellis, pointing to a closed door.

"That's where Mom sleeps," I replied. "We can go in; I don't think she'll mind."

My mother's bedroom was a tiny space, just off the living room at the front of the apartment. There wasn't room for much more than her double bed and a chest of drawers. The room didn't even have a closet. Mom kept her clothes hanging in the living room closet.

The surface of the dresser was dusty. There was a small lamp sitting there, with a dingy beige shade and a framed picture of me when I was a baby. The bed wasn't made, and the faded yellow chenille bedspread was in a tangled heap on the floor. I picked up a pillow and breathed in the scent of my mother—Dove soap, baby shampoo, and the Topaze perfume she'd bought from a door-to-door Avon lady last winter. It was the only time I'd ever seen my mother buy anything on a whim.

"Two dollars," Mom had remarked to me, although it had seemed more like she was talking to herself. The Avon lady sat on the sofa, crossing her smooth, stockinged legs, and glancing surreptitiously around the room. "I can spend two dollars on myself for once, can't I?" Mom continued, "Is it such a crime?"

The Avon lady had reached into her bag and given my mother some Soap on a Rope in a blue box. It had a cameo in the middle. The soap had a big chip out of it, and she wouldn't be able to sell it, she'd explained.

"Consider it a bonus, for your order." Mom mumbled thanks and filled in the order for the Topaze perfume. She put a drop of it behind each ear every morning when she got dressed.

I buried my face deep into the pillow. My chest tightened and the backs of my eyes stung.

"Do you think your mom would mind if we fixed up her room a little? We could make it a bit nicer for her." Ellis went to the little window and pulled the curtains apart. Rain sheeted down the glass.

"She likes flowers a lot," I said. "We could put some on the dresser. Like the ones on the kitchen table."

"That's a good idea. I'll get some more from Grammy's garden. If she likes flowers so much, I think you should draw some. We'll hang them on the walls. The walls need some pictures. And we can look in Grammy's attic for some other stuff. I'll bring it all over here Monday morning. It won't take long."

"We could draw the flowers now," I suggested. "Nothing else to do."

"We'll sit at your desk and do it," Ellis said.

Ellis dragged a chair from the kitchen into my room so she could sit next to me. I drew daisies on the drawing pad with black marker, and Ellis got a glass of water from the kitchen and dribbled water colours over them. The colours ran together and out of the edges of the flowers. Ellis held the brush filled with purple paint over her wrist and tapped it, and purple dots spattered over the page. The picture was beautiful. I picked up a paintbrush and tried to imitate her technique. We made four pictures and left them on the desk to dry.

"I thought you had to colour in the lines," I said. "All this time. I thought that was the rule."

"There are no rules in art," Ellis replied.

We put on our shoes to go to Hannah's for lunch.

I looked over at Ellis. Her long ponytail hung against her cheek as she bent over, tying her shoes. I could see little curls of dark hair hugging the nape of her neck. I reached out spontaneously and touched one of them. Ellis stood and elbowed me softly in the ribs.

When we stepped out the door, the rain had almost stopped. The few remaining drops pocked the scattered puddles on the sidewalk. The overhanging branches were dripping. Robins bobbed across lawns, shaking their wet feathers. I leaped like a gazelle over the puddles, while Ellis patiently stepped around them.

"I've got a surprise," Hannah said when we came into the kitchen. "We're going to drive uptown and have lunch at Cookie's!"

"That's where my mom works," I said.

Hannah laughed. "Yes, I know," she said. "She's expecting us. You can both order anything you like."

I felt a surge of excitement. I loved Cookie's, and it was a rare treat to go. Ellis and I ran back outside, clambered into the back of Hannah's little Volkswagen bug, and climbed over the back seat into the cubby. There we sat, with our limbs tangled up. Hannah jiggled the clutch and we went lurching through the back streets and uptown. The steadfast little VW motor hummed against our knees.

I'd been to Cookie's a few times, but never when my mother was working. Customarily, we went for lunch after back-to-school shopping (one pair of jeans, new sneakers, underwear, and five shirts— Mom would start saving after Christmas for this expenditure). Another time, we took the bus there after I'd recovered from being sick for two weeks with the red measles. (My mother had had to leave me with Cookie's sister-in-law the whole time, and promising a visit to the diner was the only way she could get me to stop crying when she left in the mornings). We always sat at the counter on spinning red-vinyl stools, sharing a plate of fries. Cookie would fill tall glasses of Coke from the fountain, with ice cubes piled to the top, and the fizzy bubbles tickled our nostrils every time we took a sip.

One time, as I sat dragging fries through a pool of ketchup, I watched Cookie behind the counter, scooping ice cream into a tall metal cup, tipping in some milk and several squirts of syrup from tall bottles. He stuck the metal cup under a rod attached to a pale green machine and pushed a button. The rod spun and beat the contents of the metal cup, and then Cookie poured the concoction into a glass—a milkshake so thick that the straw stood up in it. He brought the glass and the metal cup to a lucky kid sitting further down the counter.

The kid worked so hard at the straw that his cheeks almost turned inside-out, and when the glass was drained, he tipped the metal cup over his glass and it filled to the top again. My tongue must have been hanging out as I watched him, because Mom leaned over and whispered, "It's not polite to stare."

Crammed into the cubby of the Volkswagen bug, I decided that I would sacrifice the fries and the onion rings and the fried egg and cheese sandwiches for the divine opportunity to order a milkshake. Just thinking about it made me pant like an overheated Basset Hound. Hannah shimmied the bug into a parking space in front of the diner, and I shot out of the cubby like a cannon ball.

Cookie hobbled behind the counter, tossing burger patties onto the grill and stirring up a pile of translucent onions with his long-handled spatula. He wore his usual white T-shirt, covered in a stained apron. Cookie's wrists were perpetually striped with burns from the edge of the grill, and his bare arms were dotted with bright red marks left by spattering bacon grease.

"Hey-ya, Monkey," Cookie growled from the grill. (Cookie called all kids "monkeys.") "You folks go sit in a booth; the counter's full. I'll send Violet over in a minute."

The diner was loud and busy. The air was filled with the mingled aroma of coffee and bacon and grilled onions. Hannah slid into a seat, and Ellis and I sat across from her. Hannah took a menu and started to read through it.

"What are you having, Davy?" Ellis asked, reaching for another menu.

"Milkshake," I breathed. "Vanilla milkshake."

"You can't just have a milkshake and nothing else," Ellis noted. "Can he, Grammy?"

"He can order whatever he wants; that's what I promised," Hannah encouraged. "But David, you're welcome to order something else, too. Like a hamburger or a sandwich, maybe? How about a BLT?"

I saw my mother in her mustard-coloured waitress dress, standing at a booth a bit further down, dipping a little at the knees under a loaded tray. Mom was taking plates from the tray and leaning over the table to deliver them. Steam rose up. Her face was flushed pink, and the loose, pale hair around her face curled in the heat. The table was crowded with loud men. Construction workers.

"Hey, Violet!" one of the men exclaimed from the booth. "I ordered this sandwich toasted!"

"I'll take it back," Mom offered. "Won't take but a minute."

"I don't have time to wait," the customer grumbled. "Gotta be back to the site in fifteen minutes. Guess I'll just have to eat it the way it is. I wish you people could get an order straight once in awhile."

"Hey, don't give Violet a hard time," one of the other men said, reaching up and stroking my mother's

62

shoulder. "She's doing her best, ain't you, honey? Some girls gotta work for a living."

Seeing the man's black-rimmed cuticles sliding across my mother's shoulder made everything inside me go still and cold. The noise in the diner receded. The people faded. It was like all I could see was Mom and that man's hand. She looked suddenly like a young girl, not much older than Ellis. Not like a grown woman, not like my mother. Not like the worn-down, angry woman that had slapped me earlier that morning. Mom turned her flushed face, and we locked eyes. Then she looked away, as though she were ashamed, and turned her attention back to her customers. "Enjoy your meal, boys," I heard her say, mock-cheerful. She jammed the empty tray on her hip, squared her shoulders, and came over to our table.

"Hey, Davy," she said, one hand gripping the tray, and the other fumbling in her apron pocket for her paper pad. I looked at my mother's reddened hands and wished one of them would tousle my hair, or settle briefly on my shoulder. Even though we had hugged after our confrontation earlier that morning, there was a tangible awkwardness between us that had never been there before. "You hungry? Hello, Hannah. Hi, Ellis."

Hannah smiled broadly. "How nice to see you again, Violet. You look busy today."

Mom smiled wearily, and shrugged. "It's the usual lunch crowd, nothing out of the ordinary. It's good of you to bring Davy. He really likes it here, and he doesn't get to come often."

"It's my pleasure," Hannah replied.

"Are you all set to order?" Mom said. She looked down at me and smiled hesitantly. "Davy?"

"Could I please have a vanilla milkshake?" I dared.

Mom kept smiling, but there was a frown

underneath that I recognized right away. She wasn't happy about my request. I knew milkshakes were expensive, but I thought it would be all right since that was the only thing I was ordering. However, I couldn't risk the humiliation of explaining that to her in front of Hannah and Ellis. "Well, Davy...." She began. I felt like melting down and puddling under the table, in a soupy, sticky mess.

Hannah quickly came to my rescue and explained, "I told the kids to order whatever they liked. It's perfectly fine."

Mom's forehead creased. "I think..."

"I'll have a Coke," I said, my face flaming. I wished that I hadn't allowed myself to get so worked up about that milkshake. Even though I'd tried to remember my manners, I was still managing to be rude and inconsiderate. I hunched my shoulders.

"Oh, David, no," Hannah insisted. "Please, can you bring him the shake? I'd really like him to have it. Actually, bring three. We'll all have one. And three club sandwiches. With fries."

Mom nodded once, glanced at me, then turned and walked off with her tray.

Ellis was thumbing through the song selections in the tabletop juke box. "Do you have a dime, Grammy?" she asked.

Hannah reached into her purse. "Yes. What shall we listen to? David?"

I looked behind the counter. Cookie was scooping ice-cream into three tall metal cups, and my mother was lowering a basket of fries into the bubbling fry vat. She swatted at a loose strand of hair that had fallen out of her ponytail, then went to the fridge and yanked at the door. The construction workers got up from their table and lumbered past in their work boots on the way to the register. Mom met them at the register and tapped away at the keys. The drawer popped open with a clear ding. The men took their flattened wallets out of their back jeans pockets. Staring at my mother's back, it was almost as though I could see the man's handprint, right in that spot where she slouched a little, when she was tired. One of the men reached forward and chucked her under the chin. Mom batted his hand away and laughed.

"How about 'Little Green Apples,'" I said, my heart aching. It was the first song that came into my head. Hannah passed me the dime, and I slid it into the slot. The song started playing right away; apparently, no-one else in the diner had dimes to spare that day.

Cookie came out from behind the counter with a tray loaded with the three metal cups and three foamy glasses with straws standing at attention, and that's how the first mouthful of my milkshake tasted to me—like green apples, bitter and tongue-curdling. Like something I would never be able to swallow. But then Ellis looked at me with her calm grey eyes and gave me one of her almost-smiles as she swept her finger along the edge of the glass and licked it off. And somehow, the next mouthful went down easier. Soon, the lump in my throat was gone and the milkshake tasted how I'd imagined it would.

When lunch was over, Hannah opened her purse at the cash register and Ellis perused the mass of plants in the front window. Cookie bent his shiny head over the counter and said to me in a low voice, "You know I'm watching out for her, right, Monkey?" Then he quickly slipped me a large paper bag. My mother had her back to us at the grill. When I opened the bag in the Volkswagen's cubby a few minutes later, I discovered a white bakery box with a lid. Inside was an entire uncut coconut cream pie.

Present day

"So, did you ever find out your dad's name?" Will wonders. We are in the garage, hauling out junk for a yard sale the next day. My wife jokes that the garage has some kind of supernatural pull—a vortex that sucks all manner of junk and crap into it when she's got her head turned. I just can't seem to resist odd bits and pieces—anything that has potential to become something new, to combine or form into something functional. I disparage of abandon and uselessness.

"Grandma told me when I got older."

"What is it? What's his name?"

"Irwin. Irwin Fitz."

Will throws his head back and laughs—the hoarse, unrestrained guffaws that are typical of ten-year-old boys—the kind that involves flying spit and belly-clutching.

"Seriously?" Will finally sputters. "Irwin Fitz. Your dad's name was Irwin Fitz." He started up again, hooting and howling and wiping snot away from his nose with the backs of his hands.

"You're disgusting," I say with a bit of a smile, as I drag two old milk cans out into the front yard. "Try using a Kleenex."

"Sorry, Dad," he gasps. Will grabs another milk can and hauls it out of the garage.

We're quiet for a few minutes.

"Will," I finally say, "I never thought of Irwin Fitz as my dad."

"Did you ever try to find the guy?"

"Nah," I reply.

"Did he ever try to find you?"

"Not that I know of."

"Well, Dad," Will says. He wheels out one of the twins' old bikes and lets it fall on the grass. "Maybe Irwin Fitz started thinking about you when he got older. Maybe he was sorry he left Grandma and you the way he did."

"Maybe he grew up, you mean?"

"Yeah."

"Some people never grow up, Will," I say.

"Would you ever look for him, do you think? Aren't you curious?"

"If I needed a bone marrow transplant or something," I say, emptying a basket of nuts and bolts onto an old towel and picking through them. "Maybe then I'd try to find him. But otherwise, I think I'll just leave it alone."

"I'd be curious," Will remarks. "If it were me."

August, 1969

The afternoon after we'd eaten at the diner, I walked home from Hannah's with a heavy heart, as well as a heavy stomach. Ellis had a red rubber ball that she'd unearthed in the attic after we returned to Hannah's from Cookie's. She was tossing it high into the air and catching it cleanly in one hand as we walked along the sidewalk. I scuffed along miserably, kicking at the tufts of grass growing out of the sidewalk cracks. It was Friday, and the long hours of the weekend yawned, vast as a canyon, in front of me. I was facing two days apart from Ellis.

I put my hands across my stomach and drooped over a little. After we'd explored the attic for an hour, and the heat under the eaves drove us back down to the kitchen for cold drinks, Hannah had cut the coconut cream pie into large wedges, and we'd sat around the kitchen table, digging in. I'd explained that I couldn't bring the pie home; Cookie would catch an ear-full for giving it to me. Mom accepted leftovers from him sometimes, but hand-outs were another story.

"We can't have Cookie getting into trouble," Hannah agreed. "Let's say no more about it." She winked and passed me a plate heaped high with whipped cream and custard and toasted coconut flakes.

I couldn't remember a time when I'd ever felt that full, not even Christmas. When Mom cooked our holiday meals, she rationed things out to last over a few suppers, and I never had that experience of feeling completely stuffed. I never went hungry, but all the same, there was always an emptiness in me that wasn't quite satisfied—a voice inside my head that whispered, I wish I could have some more.

Vanilla shake and fries and club sandwich and coconut cream pie...my stomach felt like the barrel of a musket, crammed with gunpowder. One more morsel and I would explode. The walls of my stomach shifted and groaned. I sighed, and Ellis's red ball dropped smoothly into her palm.

Mom was already home—the door was unlocked, and her shoes were at the bottom of the stairs.

"See you Monday," I said to Ellis, who was leaning against the side of the house, passing the ball from one hand to the other.

Ellis stopped tossing the ball and gave me a quizzical look. "What do you mean? Are you going somewhere this weekend?"

"No. But Mom doesn't work weekends, so you don't have to come tomorrow or the next day."

"Have to come?" Ellis repeated. "What do you mean? You don't want to hang out tomorrow?"

"Yes, I do! I mean, well...sure, we could, I guess." I looked at my feet, trying to hide the grin stretching the corners of my face out of shape.

"I'll see you tomorrow. Call me."

"What, like on the phone?"

Ellis cocked an eyebrow at me. "Yes, on the phone. Your mom has Grammy's number. See you tomorrow."

I went inside and left the door open a crack so I could watch Ellis walk down the driveway. She was wearing a pair of jean shorts, cut off above the knee, and a white blouse with no sleeves and red sneakers. Her dark hair hung in two neat braids along her shoulder blades, frizzing a little in the damp.

"Tomorrow, tomorrow," I sang softly to myself, as I went down the stairs. I was ashamed to tell Ellis that I had never made a call on our telephone before. I had no one to call—no grandparents to call once a week, no friends to invite over to play. I would have to get my mother to show me how to do it.

Mom was sitting slouched at the kitchen table, with her two bare feet up on the empty chair.

"Hi, Davy," Mom yawned and filled her glass with Freshie. "Hungry?"

"No, not one bit. Can I skip supper?"

"You stuffed yourself at Cookie's today. Well, I'm not hungry, either. Let's watch a movie on the television tonight. The Incredible Mr. Limpet is on. You can stay up late to watch it. And if we're hungry, I'll make baloney and pickle sandwiches before bedtime."

"All right!" Mr. Limpet was my favourite movie of all time. Henry Limpet, played by Don Knotts, was a shy, awkward man who didn't really fit in anywhere. The only thing that brought him any joy was watching fish. Fish were his passion. One day, during a visit to Coney Island, Henry was on a dock, peering into the water, mesmerized by his beloved specimens and wishing he was one, when he toppled in. Even though his friend dove in to save him, Henry's body was never found. His wife and his friend were certain that he'd drowned, but he hadn't. He'd turned into a cartoon fish, still wearing his thick glasses, and his fishy face oddly bearing vestiges of Don Knotts. While adjusting to his dream-come-truc life and romancing the lovely Ladyfish, Henry discovered that he had a superpower—he could emit supersonic sound-waves that could blast large objects out of the vicinity, such as German U-Boats, which was very convenient at that time, as the Americans were fighting the Nazis in World War II. Mr. Limpet became a navy war hero, and forever remained what he knew he was born to be—a fish.

"I think I'll lay down for an hour," Mom yawned. "I don't want to fall asleep in the middle of the movie."

"I have some things to do," I replied. "I'll be in my room."

I pushed up the roll-top and settled at the desk. On the transistor radio by my elbow, Tommy James and the Shondells were crackling out "Crimson and Clover."

I hummed along, thinking of Ellis, and wrote a list in my best cursive of all the things we had uncovered in the attic that afternoon: old frames for the pictures we'd painted, some dusty lace curtains, a faded rag rug, a chipped ceramic jug with yellow roses painted on it, a heavy gilded hand-mirror, and some floral pillows. Those things would be for my mother's bedroom. Hannah had laundered the pillows and the curtains and the rug, and Ellis and I had hung them out earlier that afternoon on the clothesline to dry and air out. For Mr. Mosely's corner, we'd found a small glass and iron table with two ornate iron chairs. There were also two small stone rabbits and a dark green ceramic frog with most of the paint chipped off. Ellis planned to make a little sitting area, close to Mr. Mosely's back door. We would clear out the weeds and trim the bushes along the fence, tucking the rabbits into spots where they would look like they were peeking out. Ellis said she had other plans for the frog.

"Something that will help Mr. Mosely," she said, secretively.

Ellis and I dragged our treasures down the stairs, and then hauled them out to the yard where we sprayed off the dust and cobwebs with the garden hose, also managing to break several earnest truces not to spray one another.

Hannah had agreed to bring the bigger items over to my place with the Volkswagen on Monday, once my mother left for work. The other items could be put in the wagon and pulled along the sidewalk.

I wriggled in my desk chair. Monday seemed like a million years away. I flipped to a new page in my doodle pad and sketched two rabbits, crouching together in the grass.

"What have you been up to?" my mother wondered when I walked into the kitchen. She was mixing a pitcher of Freshie and heating oil on the stove for popcorn. "You've got that gleam in your eye."

"What gleam?" I responded anxiously.

Mom laughed. "I'm joking."

"I was just thinking about Mr. Mosely's corner," I said, taking the bag of popcorn kernels out of the cupboard. "We found some cool stuff in Hannah's attic this afternoon. A table and stuff."

"That's really great you and Ellis are going to do

that for Mr. Mosely," my mother said, and she pushed down on the lever of the aluminum ice-cube tray until the ice-cubes popped out and bounced all over the counter. She gathered them up and dumped them into the pitcher with the Freshie. "Maybe he'll come out of his house more if he has somewhere to go. Even if it's just his own back yard."

"Mr. Mosely has agoraphobia," I announced.

"What?" She looked over her shoulder at me.

"It's when you're afraid to leave the house. It's an illness of the mind."

"I know what it is. I'm just surprised that you do."

"I'm not a baby, Mom. I actually know a few big words. Sheesh."

"There's no need to take that tone," my mother said. "And I think you're right about Mr. Mosely." She carefully poured popcorn kernels into the hot oil and gave the pan a little shake.

"Ellis is an odd kind of girl," Mom said.

"What do you mean?"

"I don't mean it in a bad way," Mom explained. "I just mean, she's very different from other girls. Don't you think?"

"It's what I like about her." I thought of Ellis, her serious eyes, and the mouth that always seemed to stay in a straight line. Sometimes, she seemed to be on the verge of smiling, but the upward curve of her lips never quite appeared. Could a person be happy without ever smiling? I wondered.

"You like her, very much. I've noticed."

"Yeah, she's all right," I answered, shrugging. "For a girl."

"You'll be sad when she goes."

I was silent. I picked up the wooden spoon and stirred the Freshie until the ice-cubes spun around in a green whirlpool.

"She'll be going home soon," Mom continued. "You

know that, right?"

"Yes, I know," I answered quietly. "But why do I have to think about it now?"

"Sometimes, it's good to prepare ourselves for things that are going to happen," Mom answered. "Like putting plastic over the windows before the snow comes, or like stashing a bit of money away for Christmas."

"Maybe she won't go," I said. "Maybe, she'll decide to stay here with Hannah. Hannah is alone in that big house, and Ellis likes it there."

There it was. The Maybe Game again. This time, rather than a string of potential fathers, the star was Ellis.

"Davy," Mom said. "Ellis has a family and her school and friends back where she lives. She can't just leave everything behind. This is a vacation for her. Her life isn't here."

"It's seven o'clock," I mumbled. "I'm going to turn on the television."

"Bring the drinks in."

I set the glasses on the coffee table and flopped onto the couch. The opening credits for Mr. Limpet rolled across the screen. Mom came in with a big bowl and settled in beside me. We munched popcorn and gargled the shells out of our throats with green Freshie.

Near the end of the movie, Henry and his human wife arrived at the juncture in the story where they had to acknowledge the hard facts. The wife wondered, if Henry the man didn't exist anymore, did that mean she was married to a fish?.Henry explained to her that he couldn't come home with her and live in the bathtub. Under the water, Ladyfish tugged at Henry's fin. He looked tenderly at her through the thick lenses of his glasses.

I'd never felt sorry for Bessie before, and I'd seen

the movie at least half a dozen times. This time was different. Maybe Bessie could keep Henry in the bathtub. She could sit on the edge of the toilet seat and chat with him while he swam around in the tub. Every few days, she could change the water and toss in some fish food. She could even get her bathing suit on and jump in and play with him once in awhile. It could work. Maybe.

But Henry could never be happy that way. And neither could Bessie. What kind of a life was that for a fish, swimming around in a bathtub? And what would they find to talk about, when the only things in Henry's world were four smooth white walls and a bar of soap off in the distance?

I ate my baloney and pickle sandwich, and then crawled under the sheets of my bed.

Right away, I fell headlong into a watery dream. I was sitting on the sandy bottom under the sea, with silvery bubbles streaming from my mouth. "I wish, I wish, I wish I were a fish," I was thinking to myself, over and over. I raised my hands and stared at them through the murky water, still human, slightly pink. I waited for my fingers to web, to transform into fins. I waited for my skin to grow scales, for my feet to melt together into a single tail. When I realized that the transformation wasn't going to happen, my throat and lungs began to fill with water. I struggled and choked in sudden panic. My limbs thrashed in the deep water. Through the dim depths, a tail flipped, long hair trailed, and a beautiful mermaid with solemn eyes reached for me and grasped me by the shoulders, drawing me up to the surface. She tossed me onto a rock, and Mike was there, yelling at me while I floundered, coughing and gagging. The mermaid waved at me over her shoulder and disappeared under the waves with a final flick of her swirling tail. She went where I could not follow. I knew that I would never see her again.

Present day

Will and I are sitting at the kitchen table, counting up the money from the yard sale. A thrift store truck had come for what was left over—bags of the twins' cast-off clothes, a lawnmower, three outgrown bikes, a bunch of ancient tools, and some old lawn chairs. I was kind of sad to see it all go, but my wife did a little jig of happiness across the driveway as the truck pulled away. The closets are organized and the garage is tidy; you can see the cement floor, and there is room for her car to fit in once the snow starts to fly. She is one of those people who likes things to be just so. It's one of the first things that drew me to her when we met.

"You said there was more to that agoraphobic guy's story," Will says. "Hey, Dad—there's more than two hundred bucks here!"

"Splitsies," I reply. "As per our agreement."

Will grins and starts dividing the cash in half.

"Hey, don't give me all the change," I say. "So, what are you going to do with your share?"

"I'm saving it," Will responds.

I'm not surprised. My son is not miserly in any aspect of his character, except when it comes to money. "What, all of it? You're not going to buy anything?"

"Nope, it's going into the bank. What are you doing with yours?"

"I think I'll take your mom out for a nice romantic dinner," I muse.

Will makes a face. "Well, that sounds like a gigantic waste."

"Hey," I counter. "That's not a waste. That's what you call an investment."

Will rolls his eyes.

August, 1969

The mermaid dream yanked me from my sleep around dawn the following Saturday morning. I pulled on some shorts and a shirt, and went through the kitchen, past the refrigerator, which was still snoring in its night rhythm, and crept gingerly up the stairs so I wouldn't disturb my mother. She would not appreciate being wakened early on a Saturday. I had a picture of her, prowling grumpily around the kitchen in her tattered robe, simmering in her displeasure like a teabag in hot water. I carefully closed the door behind me, sat down in the driveway to put on my shoes, and then went out into the back yard to my corner.

The rising sun rinsed everything with pale light. There had been a heavy dew-fall, and each blade of grass and leaf in the back yard held a shimmering pearl of water at its edge. My sneakers were drenched as I made my way to the corner behind the shed. I swept water from the seat of the Starry Night chair and sat down on it with my drawing pad. In spite of my efforts to clear off the water, the seat of my jeans dampened instantly. I ignored it and put the drawing pad on my knees and started to sketch.

The back of the shed had an old wooden door, evidently not used in years. Vines were creeping over its surface and tall grass grew undisturbed in front of it. A rusty lift latch jutted out from behind the dripping foliage. I drew the door and sketched in the leafy vines. Birds twittered, already lively in the growing light. My eyes were drawn to the base of the lilac bush, and there, low to the ground, crouched a baby rabbit. Its whiskers trembled, and its ears stood erect. I sketched it, too. My pencil moved swiftly across the paper. Little strokes turned into the fur around the rabbit's eyes. I had never drawn so freely before, without thought. The sketch filled in right before my eyes, as though it had nothing to do with me. The rabbit remained motionless. Birds flew from the lilac bush to the roof of the shed, scolding.

"What are you doing?" a voice said suddenly.

The rabbit leapt and twisted in the air and disappeared under the bush. My mother stood there in her robe, with her arms folded across her chest and her uncombed hair tousled around her face.

I stood. "Mom, I tried to be quiet when I went outside."

"You didn't wake me," she answered. "I left the bedroom window open and the birds were making a racket. Then I went to check on you, and you weren't in your room. I figured you must be out here. What's that you're working on?"

"Oh, just a drawing."

"Will you show it to me?"

She stepped forward with her hand outstretched. I passed her the drawing pad, and she moved her hair away from her face to study it. She raised her head and looked at me. "This is really good."

"You think?"

"I do. It's hard to believe that a ten year old did something like this."

I shrugged. "I practice a lot."

Mom smiled. "I know you do. You spend a lot of time in your room, with your pencils and papers.

78

I hear the other kids out on the street, yelling and playing. But not you. Aren't you lonely?"

I looked at my mother. Her eyes were still puffy with sleep, and her fingers were pushing hair away from her face.

"Sometimes," I answered. I sat back down on the chair and opened the drawing pad. I stared down at the blank sheet of paper without really looking at it. I hadn't felt a pang of loneliness since Ellis came. I had forgotten what being lonely even felt like this past week. But a paltry few days—that was all I had left with Ellis. Then, she would be gone, and I would be back at school, the invisible boy once again.

Mom gathered the front of her robe closer. "Me, too," she said.

I gaped at her. "You're lonely?"

"I am, sometimes."

"But you've got me. And Cookie. And all those people at the diner."

"That's not the kind of loneliness that I'm talking about."

"What do you mean, then?"

"There's more than one kind of lonely," she replied. "Haven't you noticed? You don't have to be alone to feel lonely. I often feel the loneliest when I'm in a crowd of people, like on the bus, or when the diner is full of customers."

I stared at my pencil as I rolled it around between my thumb and index finger.

"Davy, would you mind if I went out on a date? I'm not asking your permission. I just want to know how you feel about it."

"What, like with a guy?"

"Yes, with a guy. A man that I like, and who likes me, wants to take me to dinner tonight. His name is Gabe Blanchard."

"Oh," I said. "Am I coming, too?" I realized as soon

as the question was out of my mouth how ridiculous
it was.

"Not this time. Actually, Hannah has invited you
to sleep over at her house tonight. She and Ellis have
pitched a tent in the back yard, and Ellis thought the
two of you could have a camp-out."

For a moment, I felt a prickle of anger rising in my
chest, colouring my cheeks. I felt as though my mother
was trying to bribe me with the prospect of a campout with Ellis so that she could get all dressed up and
perfumed and flounce off with this Gabe Blanchard
character. Then she could invite him downstairs after
their romantic dinner, and they could smooch and
cuddle and all that disgusting movie-type behaviour
without having to worry about some nuisance kid
interrupting them. I pictured my mother in her one
nice dress—yellow, with a full skirt that swirled when
she spun around, with a shiny black belt around the
waist—dancing around the apartment in the arms of
this Gabe person, who she liked and who liked her.
I imagined him dipping her down, and one of her
legs rising, so her toes pointed to the ceiling, like a
ballerina. My imagination was about to slip a rose
between Gabe Blanchard's teeth, when I called a stop
to it.

"It's fine, Mom. Have fun."

There was a pause, and then she said, "Thank
you, Davy."

"I'm kinda hungry," I said, ready to change the
subject.

"Let's go in, then. I'll make French toast."

"Mom? Will you show me how to call Ellis?" I
wondered, as we headed towards the house.

Mom looked down at me, giving me a funny look.
"What? Like on the phone, you mean?"

"Yeah."

"You don't know how to use the phone?" Her

eyebrows arched.

I shrugged. "No. I've never used it before. Who would I call?"

Mom's face went all slack and sad. "Oh, Davy."

After breakfast, Mom showed me how to use the phone that sat on an end table in the living room. The receiver was heavy, and the dial tone hummed loudly against my ear. Mom read the first number to me as I put my index finger into the dial's hole and rolled it up until it reached the metal stop. I had to start over a few times when I didn't roll the dial far enough. After I few minutes, I managed to dial all seven numbers and made contact over at Hannah's.

"Hello, Hannah Greary speaking," Hannah said in a cheerful voice.

"What do I say?" I whispered frantically to my mother.

"Say who you are and ask to speak to Ellis," Mom whispered back.

"This is Davy Barowsky, and I want to talk to Ellis now," I announced.

"Please," my mother interjected.

"Please," I added.

"Of course, David." Hannah chuckled. "I'll bring her to the phone."

Moments later, I heard Ellis's voice hum against my ear. "Hi, Davy. What's up?"

How strange to hear Ellis's voice, unattached to her person. I thought it was fantastically exciting. "Hi, Ellis!"

"My God, it's like you're Alexander Graham Bell the first time he realized his invention worked." My mother laughed.

"What?" I glared at my mother. How did anyone expect me to listen to two people at once?

Ellis's voice tickled my ear. "Want me to come over?"

"Yes, come over!"

"Davy, you don't have to shout. I can hear you fine. Just talk normal," Ellis's voice coaxed.

"Oh."

"See you in a few minutes. Bye," Ellis said.

I'd seen my mother hang up the phone many times. I jammed it onto the cradle, causing the phone to jangle a little.

"How was that?"

"Good. But next time, make sure you say good-bye. Otherwise people will think you're hanging up on them. It's rude."

"Ellis won't think I'm rude," I defended myself with a great deal of indignation.

I went up the stairs and positioned myself at the door to wait. Sure enough, there was Ellis, coming up the driveway, just like she'd said. I leaped out the door and waved at her frantically, as though I hadn't seen her in months.

"I'm glad to see you, Ellis," my mother said when we walked into the kitchen. "I meant to pay you yesterday." She went to the kitchen counter and grabbed her purse, an old black patent leather thing she'd had for years. The leather had hardened and cracked, and one of the handles had come away.

"That's all right," Ellis said hurriedly. "You don't have to pay me, Mrs. Barowski."

"It's Miss," my mother corrected. "And of course, I'm going to pay you. You've done an excellent job taking care of Davy. And this was a good week for tips." She handed Ellis a twenty, a ten, and five one dollar bills. "Seventy-five cents an hour," Mom said. "That should be right."

"That's thirty-five bucks!" I exclaimed.

"That's too much," Ellis protested.

"Dammit, you're rich, Ellis," I bellowed.

"Davy, watch your mouth," my mother snapped.

"No, Ellis. It's not too much. I wish it were more." She glared at me. "Trust me, I know you've earned it."

That afternoon, Ellis and I got started on Mr. Mosely's corner.

"I th-think there's an old push mower in the sh-shed," he told us when he answered our knock at his door. "I haven't b-been in there in a l-long time. It should be n-near the front."

"Will you show us?" Ellis said.

Mr. Mosely's shoulders sank noticeably. "Not this t-time," he mumbled. "Here's the k-key."

Ellis and I went back to the shed and unlocked the front door. That cool, musty smell reminiscent of old cellars and unaired rooms wafted into our nostrils. My eyes squinted in the dim light. There were old wheelbarrows and spades, tin watering cans and a cement birdbath, all swathed in dust and cobwebs. The push mower was near the front, as Mr. Mosely had thought—smooth wooden handles and metal wheels. The blades were still clogged with withered grass. I wondered how many years it had been since that grass had been caught there. I had no memory of the lawn ever being cut, and I'd lived in that house my whole life. I grasped the handles and rolled the mower outside while Ellis struggled with the bird bath. The metal table with its two matching chairs sat at the end of the driveway where Hannah had delivered them, along with the frog and the two stone rabbits.

Ellis and I hosed off the mower's blades. It took the two of us to push it through the tall grass and weeds. The blades spun and struggled during the battle, clogging up repeatedly. All we wanted was a little patch of green between the back door and the side fence, but it took two hours. Sweating profusely, I got a rusty garden rake out of the shed and dragged it through the thick carpet of clippings. Ellis and I carried armloads to the garbage cans.

"We'll do some more on Monday," Ellis said. The entire front of her old T-shirt was stained with grass and mud. Mine was no better. In fact, it was worse. "We need to go to Grammy's and get organized for tonight."

The tent in Hannah's yard was a heavy brown thing. The flaps had been lowered away from the windows, but it was stifling and close inside, and the air was heavy with the smell of hot, damp canvas. I lay down on the floor on top of the sleeping bag Hannah had found for me and stared up at the apex where poles met at the ceiling. The shadows of leaves dappled across the tight canvas. Ellis lay down beside me. A summer breeze dipped through the trees, breathing heavy, then stilled. The birdsong dwindled. Ellis and I lay, quiet. After a few minutes, I stole a glance at her. Her eyes were closed, and her hands were motionless on her stomach. There was a little smear of grass on her cheekbone, near her eyelid.

"What are you looking at?" she blurted suddenly, without opening her eyes.

I quickly twisted my head away. "Nothing. Your eyes are closed. Why do you think I'm looking at you?"

"I always know when someone's looking at me," Ellis replied. "I have a sense about it."

"That's weird."

Ellis opened her eyes, rolled over, and looked across at me. "I'm not your average bear. Haven't you noticed?"

I smiled, but didn't reply.

Ellis sat up and hugged her knees. "I forgot to tell you. I have a friend coming over tonight. She's camping out, too. And she's bringing her little brother."

"There isn't room," I snapped.

That was terrible news. I didn't want anyone intruding on my night in the tent with Ellis. I wanted it to be just the two of us. I'd imagined us whispering until dawn. I wanted her to tell me her secrets. I wanted to stay awake after she drifted off and watch her when she slept. I wanted to listen to her breathing. I wanted to compare our dreams in the morning.

"Davy, there's lots of room," Ellis said, frowning at me. "This is a six-man tent. It'll be fun! We'll stay up late and eat chips and drink all the pop we want."

"Who are these people?"

"Sylvia's family goes to Grammy's church. I've been to Sunday school with her a few times. And her brother is the same age as you. I thought it would be fun for you to play with someone your own age. His name is Richard."

In my mind, I wandered the rows of my Grade Three classroom, searching for a Richard. If the kid was my age, chances were he'd been in my class at school. There were only two schools in the town we lived in—the public and the Catholic. I didn't recall any Richards or Ricks or Rickys in my class. Still, the prospect of being forced to play with this kid threw me into stomach-flopping despair. As I fumbled silently through my options, I realized quickly that I didn't have any. My mother was going on some dinner date and had arranged for me to be elsewhere. I couldn't opt to stay home.

Dammmmmiit, my brain seethed.

The front flaps of the tent opened, and Hannah's round face appeared. "Who wants lemonade?"

I climbed to my feet. "I have to go," I said. "I'll be back with my pillow and stuff later."

As I trudged along the sidewalk, I wondered about this friend of Ellis's. She'd never mentioned any Sylvia to me before. Maybe, she'd been hanging around with this girl in the evenings, once she was done minding me. I imagined Ellis and Sylvia, draped across Ellis's bed, looking at beauty magazines, talking about boys, experimenting with makeup, and doing each other's hair. Giggling. All those girlie things I'd thought were beneath Ellis. I scowled. Ellis and Sylvia had conspired to bring this Richard kid along so that I would be busy playing with him and would stay out of their hair. Ellis probably didn't even want me there tonight. It was easy to conjure up a battle scene between Ellis and her grandmother. "You told Violet WHAT?" Ellis would have shrieked. "I have to have Davy all night? But you told me I could have Sylvia over for a campout! Now I'm stuck with Davy? I'm stuck with him all week as it is! This isn't fair!"

I flushed with humiliation, just thinking of it.

Down in the apartment kitchen, my mother was busy at the counter. The room was warm and smelled of sugar and butter. "Hey, Davy," she greeted. "Look, I made you something for your campout tonight."

She moved aside to reveal a tray of cupcakes slathered with chocolate frosting. "Here," she said, handing me a little jar. "I thought you would like to decorate them. There are some sprinkles inside."

"I didn't know you knew how to make cupcakes," I remarked, as I unscrewed the top of the jar.

Mom gave me a sharp look and smoothed the front of her apron. "I've made cupcakes before. Haven't I?"

"No." I shook sprinkles lavishly over the cupcakes. The only time I'd ever had cupcakes was when some kid in my class was having a birthday, and his mother had made enough for the whole class. The popular kids would get the best ones, and I would get the runt, or the one that was caving in or starting to break apart. Mom didn't send treats to school for my birthday. I didn't ask her to. I knew she couldn't afford the expense, and I didn't want the awkward task of distributing them to the other kids. They probably would have turned their noses up anyway.

"Well," Mom said. "Then it's high time, isn't it?"

"Thanks, Mom. They look really good."

"There's plenty for everyone. Hannah told me there will be some other kids there, too. It'll be like a party!" She smiled brightly.

"I'm going to pack my stuff for tonight." I went into my room and softly shut the door. The transistor radio was laying on my desk, and I turned it on. Bob Dylan's twangy voice sang "Stay, Lady, Stay" between the waves of crackling static.

I stuffed my pajamas and a clean shirt for the morning into a paper bag . I looked at Boo, with his tattered ears spread across my pillow. I had planned to leave him at home but spontaneously grabbed him and stuffed him deep down inside my pillowcase. I expected there would be some lonely times ahead in the night to come.

Present day

"What happened to that old radio?" Will says. We're sitting on the front porch, waiting for my wife to come home with a pizza. "Do you still have it?"

"I don't know where it got to," I reply. "It never worked all that well any way. It probably broke and got tossed out." I smile. "I kept the best part, though."

"What part?"

"The music. Elvis. The Beatles. Connie Francis. The Hollies. Soundtrack of my brain."

"Dad. That's fogey music. What about the rabbit? Did that get tossed out, too?"

I smile. "I think I still have old Boo somewhere. What's left of him."

The last time I'd seen Boo, he'd been stuffed into a dusty box in the back of a closet with some old books. My wife was pregnant with Will and I'd been looking through the twins' old baby things. Seeing Boo's drooping, faded ears, I'd picked him up and given him a sniff, but his reassuring scent was long gone. He was stiff and rough, all the softness lost. I should have tossed him out but in the end, I'd set him on top of the box before I closed the closet doors.

"Dad," Will says. "I like this story about the summer you were my age, but I have to tell you. You're getting side-tracked too much. I wonder sometimes if you have ADD. And also, there's too much mushy crap."

"Mushy crap?"

"It's not normal to fall in love when you're ten," Will says. "You should have been happy about those other kids coming on the campout. Not jealous."

"It wasn't that kind of love, Will," I explain. "It was connection. That's how it starts."

"Sounds like love to me," Will observes. "And it's pretty gross. You can just skip over the romantic crap and stick to the story. If you don't mind."

"In fact, I do mind. It's my story, and I don't remember taking you on as my editor. If you want to hear it, then you'll have to take the good with the bad. At least, your interpretation of the bad."

"I already know how this story ends," Will reminds me.

"Please allow me the opportunity to colour it in a little," I reply. "A story is more than an ending. And you think I have ADD?" I grin.

August, 1969

Mom walked me back over to Hannah's for the camp-out. She was dressed for her date; her high heels clicking against the sidewalk as we hustled along. A breeze riffled through the full skirt of her yellow dress, and the sweet scent of her Topaze teased my nostrils. Balanced in her hands in front of her was the tray of cupcakes. She had gathered her hair back into a smooth bun at the nape of her neck, but a strand had worked its way loose and was falling across her eyes. Since her hands were full, she kept contorting her mouth and blowing air up at it so that it would move out of the line of her vision. My hand twitched, wanting to brush it away for her, but she looked so beautiful and unfamiliar; I suddenly felt too shy to touch her.

89

"Violet, how lovely you look," Hannah exclaimed at the front door. She took the tray of cupcakes and headed towards the kitchen, inviting us to follow. "Davy, Ellis is in the tent. Go on out."

Mom bent to give me a quick hug. "Bye, Davy," she said. "Behave yourself."

Hannah had her back to us at the sink. I threw my arms around my mother's neck and gave her a fierce, quick hug.

"Sheesh, Davy," she whispered, and smiled. "It's not like I'm going on a European tour. It's just a dinner date. I'll see you in the morning."

Out in the yard, there were voices coming from the tent. My heart sank. I'd been holding out hope that Sylvia and Richard would be no-shows. Obviously, the stars had aligned against me.

Ellis poked her head out of the tent. "Oh, Davy. There you are," she said. "We've been waiting for you. Come on in and see what we did." She held the tent flap up and I crept under her arm and inside.

The interior of the tent looked nothing like the last time I'd seen it, earlier that afternoon. Streamers were wound around the poles, paper chains hung from the roof poles, and the floor was littered with balloons. A black-eyed little boy sat cross-legged on a sleeping bag, blowing a noise maker. It shrieked, shot out straight, and then curled up like a snake, over and over. The boy waved at me and blasted the noise-maker again. The girl, Sylvia, was sitting, too, making tissue flowers and tossing them into a pile beside her. Her left leg was as straight as a poker, encased in a cumbersome metal brace. A crutch lay beside her.

"This is Davy," Ellis told them.

"Is it someone's birthday?" I said, gazing around me.

Sylvia shook her head. "Hannah gave us this stuff to play with. Party tent. Ellis's idea."

Sylvia's eyes were black, like her brother's. They gazed frankly out from under a fringe of curly dark bangs, past the spray of freckles across her nose. The leg inside the brace was frighteningly shriveled and thin—a stark contrast to the normal one beside it. It looked dead. I couldn't tear my eyes off it, and Sylvia noticed.

"I had polio," she said. "When I was two. I can walk with the brace and the crutch. But the leg will never get better. I was in an iron lung for five months. I'm not retarded, and I don't need to go to a special school. I just have a bum leg. That's it. Any more questions, ask them now so we can get it over with. I don't want to talk about polio all night."

I had plenty of questions toppling over one another in my head. Does it hurt? How does an iron lung work? Do you take the brace off when you go to bed? Will the brace rust if you get it wet?

However, none of those concerns held a candle to my biggest one, which reared up suddenly and staggered through my mind like Bigfoot. The monster crashed through the underbrush of my brain matter and thudded against the walls of my skull. Sylvia was going to give me polio. And Ellis was going to catch it, too.

Ellis scooped the pile of tissue flowers that Sylvia had made off of the floor of the tent and tucked them into the paper chains. Busy making everything pretty, as usual. I felt an overwhelming wave of annoyance wash over me. Was that all Ellis ever thought about, her stupid corners?

You're one of her corners, a little voice in my head said, clear as a bell. She finds messed up things and tries to fix them. Sylvia is one of those messed up things. And so are you.

I looked at Richard, who was idly batting away at one of the paper chains hanging down near his ear.

91

She's even found you a friend, the voice continued. A boy your own age. Someone for you to play with, so you can feel normal.

I dropped my paper bag of stuff in the corner and sank down beside it. Ellis lifted her face and studied me. "What's wrong, Davy?"

"I have a headache," I replied, in a small voice. I wasn't exactly lying. My horror of catching polio, and my sudden inkling that I was one of Ellis's special projects, were collectively making my head spin.

"Grammy has some Aspirin in the house. Go ask her for some." A breeze came through the window flap and made the paper chains dance a little. Ellis looked at them with satisfaction.

"Will you come with me?" As frightened as I was, coupled with the strange kind of annoyance I felt with Ellis at that moment, my mission was set out before me. I had to save us from catching polio. The only way I could do that without risking her outrage was to find ways to keep us separated from Sylvia.

"All right. We'll be right back," she said to Sylvia and Richard.

The sun was well behind the trees. It was that magic time, where the last slants of the summer light edge everything with gold. I could smell cut grass and the pungent odour of Hannah's tomato plants.

"I see lots of ripe tomatoes," I said, as we passed the garden. "Let's pick them for your grandmother before we go in."

Ellis raised her eyebrows. "That doesn't have to be done right now. I don't want to keep Sylvia and Richard waiting. Besides," she added. "You should take some Aspirin before your headache gets worse."

Hannah was sitting on the back patio with her tea, enjoying the sunset. "Hello, you two," she said. "How are things going in the party tent?"

"Fine," Ellis replied. "But Davy has a headache.

92

Can I give him an Aspirin?"

"There are some children's Aspirins up in the bathroom cabinet," Hannah said. "Are you feeling sick, David?"

"Yes," I announced. "I am." I clutched my stomach for effect.

"Come here," Hannah said, motioning me over. She laid a hand on my forehead. "You don't seem warm at all."

"I'll get the Aspirin," Ellis said.

"No, I'll do it," I almost shouted.

"Bring it to me when you find it!" Hannah called after me.

I ran into the house and up the stairs. I found myself in front of Ellis's bedroom door again—firmly shut. My hand reached out, as though it had a mind all its own, and grasped the white ceramic doorknob. I looked around me, cautiously. No one was in the house. No one would know if I just took a peek. I so badly wanted to know what Ellis's bedroom looked like, to see the books she was reading, to see the pictures hanging on the walls, to touch the bed where she slept every night...to see what kind of corner she had created for herself in there.

I just don't like it when anyone goes in there, I heard Ellis whisper, inside my head.

I jerked my hand away from the doorknob. "Fine then, dammit," I muttered, and stomped off down the hall to the bathroom. The bottle of pink children's Aspirin was sitting on the middle shelf of the medicine cabinet. I grabbed it and shoved it under the billowing crocheted dress of the doll that sat on the tank of the toilet. Sure enough, the next roll of toilet paper was tucked under the pink layers of the dress, ready to replace the present one. Mom kept one of these things on our toilet, too. Ours had skirts that were bright green, and the eyes of the cheap doll were crossed.

Cookie had given it to Mom as a Christmas gift one year. Sometimes, I grabbed it and poked it in the eyes while I was sitting on the toilet.

I peered through the bathroom window, which overlooked the patio. Hannah was still sitting in the chair with her cup, and Ellis stood beside her, waiting patiently. I closed the lid of the toilet and sat down on it. I wondered what an iron lung looked like. I imagined something massive—reddish-pink and purple-veined, expanding and shrinking as air rushed in and out. At the top, I envisioned my head jutting out, the rest of me swallowed up inside the lung, unable to breathe or squirm. In my imagination, the lung morphed into a stomach. Inch by inch, my head dropped lower inside it, until I was swallowed altogether. The lung shuddered and belched with great satisfaction. Beside it, stood another lung, quivering gelatinously. Ellis's head was sticking out of that one, thrashing and twisting as she screamed, over and over...

I hung my head and hugged my arms around myself. Several minutes later, I heard footsteps on the stairs, and I quickly stood up and went back over to the open medicine cabinet.

"Did you find it?" Hannah said.

"No," I answered, mustering up consternation in my voice and trying to look confused. "I've looked everywhere, but I just don't see it."

Hannah came over and started moving things aside in the cabinet. "That's odd," she said, frowning. "I know I just put a new bottle in here the other day..."

I felt a stab of guilt. I did not enjoy deceiving Hannah this way, especially since she had been so good to me. But I had to focus on the important thing here. And that was to keep Ellis and myself out of polio's way.

"Well, I'll slip down to the store and buy some more," Hannah said, shutting the cabinet door. "You go on back to the tent. I sent Ellis back there a few minutes ago."

"What!" I shouted. "She's back in the tent?"

Hannah startled. I rushed past her to the bathroom door, but she caught my arm.

"David! What on earth is wrong with you?"

I looked into Hannah's kind face. I was so choked with agitation that I couldn't speak.

"Do you really have a headache?"

I shook my head.

"Ahhh," she said. "Don't you like Sylvia and Richard? Are you maybe a little jealous? Ellis is paying too much attention to them and not enough to you?"

"It's not that," I protested.

"What is it, then?"

I swallowed and looked away. "It's the polio," I finally managed to say.

"The polio?" Hannah repeated. "Sylvia, you mean? Does her leg bother you?"

"Well, yes," I admitted. "But that's not it, exactly."

Hannah raised her shoulders and lifted her palms. Waiting for an answer.

"I don't want to catch it! And I don't want Ellis to catch it, either."

Hannah's eyes widened. She lowered herself down and sat on the edge of the tub. "Oh, David. That's what this is all about? Where did you put the Aspirin?"

I sighed. "Under the toilet paper doll."

Hannah drew me over to her and lay her hands on my shoulders. "Do you think I would expose you or Ellis to any danger? Look at me."

I raised my eyes.

"Do you think I would invite Sylvia over here if there were any chance that someone could contract the polio virus? Think about it. Does that make any sense?"

I shrugged.

"Sylvia is not contagious, David. She was when she first had polio, ten years ago. But not anymore. There is no way on earth you could catch polio from her. I am one hundred percent positive that you and Ellis will not catch polio from Sylvia tonight."

"Don't tell Ellis," I begged. "She'll think I'm stupid."

"Ellis would never think you're stupid. But I promise this chat will remain between us. Now, please go put the Aspirin back where it belongs."

The four of us played ManHunt when it got dark. Sylvia was remarkably stealthy, in spite of the brace and the crutch, and her strange, hop-drag run was faster than mine. She caught me in her arms several times, while I screamed and laughed and struggled. We played Hands Down in the tent while the Coleman lantern hissed on the floor beside us. Richard's face looked ghoulish in the lantern light. His mouth was ringed black with chocolate frosting.

"You look creepy, Richard," Sylvia laughed. "I wish we had a Ouija board."

"What's a Ouija board?" I wondered.

Richard's face was grim and pale in the dim light. "You talk to dead people with it," he said, in a low voice.

I shivered. "For real? Like, you hear their voices?"

Sylvia shook her head. "No. Everybody puts their hands on this triangle thing and it points to letters. The spirits spell out messages."

"Is there one in your grandmother's attic?" I said to Ellis.

Her eyes were downcast. She fiddled with a tissue flower that had fallen to the floor. "No," she said, abruptly. "And besides, I don't think that's a very good game."

"It's fun," Sylvia said. "We've played it at our cousins' house. It's not like the spirits are really talking to you. I don't think."

"I don't know anyone that's dead anyway," I said. "Well, just Cookie's wife, but I never met her."

"Our grandfather died before I was born," Richard said. "But what would he say to me? He never even knew me."

"I hardly remember him," Sylvia said. "He probably wouldn't have much to say to me, either. What about you, Ellis? Do you know anyone who died?"

Ellis lifted her face. Her eyes were huge and hollow-looking in the shadows. For a moment, our eyes met. She had the look of a captive being held in some terrible, secret place, and she'd just spotted me, hidden and watching from behind a bush. Help, her enormous eyes pleaded, silently. Help me.

"I'm hungry," I blurted suddenly.

"Dave," said Richard. Apparently, Davy wasn't cool enough for him. "You just ate a Sweet Marie, a huge bowl of ice cream, a whole box of Good and Plenty, and two and a half cupcakes." Richard had dispatched the other half of that cupcake personally, and that was after he'd eaten three whole ones.

If I'd been using my head, I might have made another hasty comment, such as "I have to pee really bad" or "Let's play another round of Hands Down" or "Anyone ever seen The Incredible Mr. Limpet?" Anything that wasn't related to the issue of hunger. The over-crammed feeling I'd had after the lunch at Cookie's was nothing compared to this. It felt like sugar was oozing out of my eardrums.

"Thanks for noticing, Richard," I said.

Ellis reached behind her for the carton of ice-cream. "There's lots left," she said. "You might as well eat it before it melts."

"Anyone else want some?" I asked, hopefully.

Sylvia and Richard groaned, but Ellis picked up a spoon. "I'll help you with it," she said. In the dark, her hand crept along the floor and lay atop of mine for a moment before she pulled it away again.

Even though her hand was gone, I could feel it there still, a phantom warmth and softness. As curious as I was, I knew then that to ask her would be a betrayal. Whatever it was that had happened to Ellis, she did not want to talk about it. If she did, she would have told me long ago.

Sometime after midnight, we all lost steam and crawled into our sleeping bags. Moonlight streamed in through the open window flaps. Ellis rolled over to face me. Her dark hair fanned out over her pillow. Her eyes—in the shadows and silvery moonlight—were luminous and sad. Near the front of the tent, Richard snored softly. Sylvia had unstrapped the leg brace and it was lying on the floor of the tent, near her head. It didn't look so ominous when it was empty; just a heap of metal and hinges.

"Ellis?" I whispered.

"What?" she whispered back.

"Can people be corners?"

Ellis frowned a little, looking thoughtful. After a moment, she said, "No...I don't think so. Corners are something you fix up...and sometimes, you can't fix people."

I should have felt relieved, but instead I felt an aching grief clutching at my heart. "Sometimes, you can," I suggested, hopefully. "Maybe?"

Ellis said nothing. I reached down into my sleeping bag until my hand closed over Boo.

"Here," I whispered, softly enough so that only she could hear. "This will help you sleep."

Ellis's hand reached out, and I pushed the stuffed rabbit into it.

Ellis put Boo on her pillow, next to her face. "Thanks, Davy," she whispered. She closed her eyes then, and soon, I could hear the soft rhythm of her sleep-breathing. The moon swam slowly across the sky, leaving the tent in deep shadow. When I couldn't see Ellis's face any longer, I closed my eyes and let myself fall away into the sad darkness.

Present day

"So," Will says from the back seat as we drive towards the soccer field. "That dinner date of Grandma's. That was Grandpa?"

I nod. "That was him. Grandma met him at Cookie's when he stopped by for lunch one day. He was a travelling salesman back then."

"What did he sell?"

"Vacuum cleaners."

"That sounds pretty boring."

I glance in the mirror at my son. He has the window rolled down half-way, and his dark curls are caught the wind. His face looks serene, like his mother's. It startles me sometimes, to see glimpses of my wife in the form of a ten-year-old boy.

"It wasn't boring to your grandmother," I reply.

After that first date, Gabe Blanchard had found many creative ways to rearrange his sales route so that it went past our door. Many times, he came unannounced. I would climb the stairs and answer the door to find him there, standing stiff and tall in his suit jacket and tie, with his thick hair swept back away from his face into a peak over his forehead, like James Dean.

"Would your mother happen to be at home?" he would ask formally.

"She's home," I would reply.

Feet would be scurrying, and dresser drawers

would be slamming beneath us. The sounds of her distress were so obvious to me, although I don't think Gabe had an inkling of the tizzy into which his arrival had thrown my mother. I would lead Gabe into the kitchen and pour him a glass of ice water. He sat at the table and sipped at his water patiently until Mom breezed into the kitchen in fresh clothes, hair perfectly arranged, and two fresh drops of Topaze dabbed behind her ears. Behind her closed bedroom door, I knew the contents of her drawers were strewn from one corner of the room to the other, the result of her frantic rampage.

On those visits, Gabe would take the two of us out to the drive-in for hamburgers and onion rings, or to a movie. Each time we got into Gabe's car, Mom would sit progressively closer to him up in the front seat while I found a spot to worm into in the back between the hoses and nozzles and vacuum cleaner attachments. Gabe flicked on the radio, and we sang along with Creedence Clearwater Revival and the Everly Brothers. I think my mother and I knew that Gabe was the one when we reached the point where we were comfortable singing at the top of our lungs in Gabe's car. It happened awfully fast.

Gabe found a job managing a department store in his hometown before he proposed to my mother. He didn't think a travelling man had the right to suggest marriage. When Mom told Cookie she was quitting to get married, she almost changed her mind when he started crying over the grill.

"It's the damn onions," he'd shouted at her when she'd tried to hug him. Then, seeing her slumped shoulders, he'd thrown his arm around her and told her he was going to give her an engagement party in the diner and invite the whole damned town.

Going to that party was one of the last things we did before we moved away from there. I remember that

Hannah came to that, although Ellis couldn't make the trip back. The diner was so packed that people spilled out into the streets. All the regulars had taken up a collection, and there was enough money there for them to go on a honeymoon in Florida.

I stayed with Gabe's parents for a week while they were gone. Their names were Dorcas and Mort, but they quickly became Gram and Gramps—not just because their Christian names were rather unfortunate, but because the two of them became real grandparents to me, and to my younger sisters when they came along. They babysat us, spoiled us, took us camping, snuck us candy, bought us inappropriately loud toys—all those myriad things that grandparents were created to do. God bless them both.

I had been fatherless all my life, up until Gabe Blanchard came along. When we first talked about Gabe adopting me, I worried that I would be unable to get the word Dad to sound natural in my mouth. I only had to practice it once. After that, I didn't give it another thought. The transition from Gabe to Dad was instantaneous.

August, 1969

The Monday morning after the campout, when my mother had left for the bus, I followed Ellis into my mother's room and watched her work her magic. She put me to work getting the pictures frames unfastened and putting our flower art inside while she took down the dingy curtains and replaced them with the freshly laundered lace ones from Hannah's attic. I tugged away at the sheets on the bed and threw the new bedspread on top, then arranged the floral cushions. Ellis drove a few nails into the walls and hung the pictures. We set the jug on the dresser, which Ellis had filled with daisies and snapdragons from Hannah's garden, and lay the rag rug beside the bed.

We stood at the door, looking around the room. "It's girly," I finally said.

Ellis gave me a little shove. "Your mother is a girl, in case you didn't notice."

"Yeah. She will love this."

Ellis's eyebrows drew together. "I hope she won't be upset that we were in here."

"She won't," I assured her, but I wasn't so sure myself. Mom's moods were unpredictable. I couldn't imagine her not liking the surprise we'd put together, but Ellis might be right—maybe she wouldn't like her privacy being invaded.

We headed over to Hannah's for a quick lunch, and then doubled back to finish the rest of Mr. Mosely's corner. As we tore weeds and grass away from the fence, our fingers snagged on some thorns. There were several rose bushes against the fence that we hadn't noticed, choked and hidden by weeds. The bushes were bedraggled and bare, but leaves uncurled along the branches in spots.

"Grammy would know what to do with these," Ellis said, sucking on a finger. "She's good with roses. I think they need to be cut back or something."

"I th-think I could handle that," said Mr. Mosely from the door. "If one of you would b-be so k-kind as to f-fetch the c-clippers from the shed."

Mr. Mosely stepped gingerly out of the door and stood there, looking anxiously around. "You've made a l-lot of p-progress with this c-corner," he said.

"I'll get the clippers," Ellis volunteered.

"There should be g-garden gloves in there, too," he called after her.

Mr. Mosely ventured over to the fence. "I'd f-forgotten about M-Mother's roses," he said, tracing the edge of a leaf with the tip of his finger. "She t-took such pride in them. The white ones were her f-favourite."

"They could be nice again," I suggested. "If you took care of them."

Mr. Mosely looked at me and shook his head. "I'm afraid it all got to be j-just a little t-too much for me."

Ellis came back with the clippers and the gloves and handed them to Mr. Mosely. While he chopped weakly away at the rose bushes, cutting away the dead wood, Ellis and I tackled the bricked barbecue pit, filling another garbage can with blackened cans and charred sticks. After that was done, we went to fetch the little iron table and chairs from the driveway. We arranged them close to the back door, in the shade.

Mr. Mosely straightened. "Where did those c-come from?"

"Just some old stuff my grandmother had in her attic. She was glad to get rid of it," Ellis replied. "It's pretty old, but it's sturdy. Maybe you could come out and sit back here sometimes."

Mr. Mosely lay the clippers in the grass and made his way over to one of the chairs. He lowered himself into it and stretched his legs out into a patch of sunshine. Ellis and I bent to arrange the little stone rabbits, and then Ellis went to the driveway to retrieve the green frog. Mr. Mosely's eyelids drifted shut. I stared at him. His face was terribly pale and drained. Like a vampire, I thought, that creeps into a coffin and hides from the sun all day. I shuddered a little, but then Mr. Mosely opened his eyes and looked over at me and smiled a little.

Ellis came back with the green ceramic frog clutched in her arms.

"You wouldn't want to drop that on your foot," Mr. Mosely said. "Who's this f-fellow?" He bent forward for a closer look.

"The wandering frog," Ellis said.

"The wandering f-frog? Why wandering?" Mr. Mosely frowned a little.

"He'll move on if you don't touch him every day," Ellis replied. I almost laughed, but she caught my eye, and I could see that she was very serious. I clamped my jaws shut and cleared my throat.

"Oh," Mr. Mosely said speculatively. "This wandering frog, he's the s-sensitive type, is he?"

"He just needs a little attention," Ellis explained. "He's not all that much trouble, really."

"I see."

"He just doesn't like it when people forget about him. He was pretty miserable in Grammy's attic. If the door wasn't always shut, he would've made a run for it years ago."

Mr. Mosely stared at the frog. "I'll d-do my best to k-keep him around." He reached out and ran his finger along the frog's smooth back.

Ellis took the frog and set it in the grass, a few feet away from his chair. Mr. Mosely gave it a wary look, as though he expected the frog to make its move towards the gate.

I wandered further into the yard, where the grass and weeds were still tall. The branches of the weeping willow drooped heavily, fronds of leaves touched the ground. I swept them aside and went under the tree. No grass grew here—the sun had not permeated this spot in years. Layers of dead leaves were spongy under my feet, and the ground was littered with broken branches.

The tree's apex was low to the ground, so I climbed into the spot where the massive branches forked apart and sat there, in the willow's lap. I lifted my face to stare into the tree's distant crown. Slightly above me, I noticed a flash of red. I climbed to my feet and leaned against the rough bark of the tree, reaching for it. The object was wedged in tightly between two branches, but I tugged and managed to wrest it free. After all my effort, I was disappointed. It was just an old yo-yo. I tipped it over and dirty water dribbled out. The string broke when I tugged on it, rotted right through.

I climbed down from the tree and brought the yo-yo over to Mr. Mosely. "Look what I found in the tree," I said, extending my palm to show him.

Mr. Mosely's eyes widened. "I h-haven't seen that in years." He took the yo-yo from my hand and brought it close to his face, as though he wanted to smell it or rub it against his cheek. He looked like a kid who'd just found a dollar on the sidewalk.

"Was it yours?" I said.

"No. No, it-it was my brother's," Mr. Mosely said, turning the yo-yo around in his hand, still peering closely at it.

"Maybe he'd like to have it back," I suggested. "He could put a new string in it."

Then, like a cloud passing over the sun, Mr. Mosely's face darkened. "My b-brother died when he was five."

I looked quickly over at Ellis. Her face was sober and pale. She didn't meet my eyes.

I moved closer to Ellis, feeling suddenly exposed and uncertain. A part of me wanted to hear about what had happened to Mr. Mosely's brother, but at the same time, there was nothing I wanted more than for him to stop talking.

Mr. Mosely carefully set the yo-yo on the table. His palm hovered over it for a moment, and then he stood up.

"It's g-good of you k-kids," he said, "t-to do this for m-me. I h-have to go in now." He darted inside so quickly, we didn't have a chance to say good-bye.

For several moments, Ellis and I were completely still, holding our breaths.

Then, I exhaled loudly. "Do you think that's why he stays in his house all the time? Because of his brother?"

Ellis shook her head. "That's probably one of the reasons. There're probably lots of reasons." She went to the table and picked up the yo-yo.

"Don't touch it," I said, shuddering. "That's a dead kid's yo-yo. Creepy."

Ellis raised her eyes and stared at me angrily. For a moment, I wondered if she was going to yell at me. I supposed I'd said something stupid or irritating or thoughtless. I felt my face go hot.

But Ellis dropped her gaze and set the yo-yo back on the table. She went over to the frog and stooped down, laying her hands on its head.

"Every morning," Ellis instructed me, "When you come outside, come back here and move the frog a few inches away from the chair."

"But, Ellis," I ventured. "Mr. Mosely is a grown-up. He's not going to believe the frog is coming to life at night and hopping around."

"Of course he's not," Ellis returned. "But hopefully, he'll be coming out here every day to touch the frog. And if you move it a little further away from the house over time, Mr. Mosely will have to come a little further, too."

"Oh..." I breathed. "I get it."

I recalled that Mr. Mosely had been in the back corner of the yard, where Ellis and I had made the lilac bush fort, but he'd been shaking and miserable the entire time. How did someone get over agoraphobia? Was it even possible? Maybe it was, if you took it slow. One step, one touch. One corner at a time.

Ellis went to the table and slipped on the gardening gloves discarded by Mr. Mosely. Then she bent to pick up the dead rose clippings. I sat beside the frog and watched her. My fingers stroked the top of the frog's cool, smooth head. The shade lengthened across the yard, and the willow tree sighed in the breeze. Ellis put the clippers and gloves back in the shed and sank onto one of the iron chairs.

I rolled back into the grass onto my side and shaded my eyes with my arm. It looked like I was drowsing, but I was watching Ellis from under the crook of my arm. I hoped she wouldn't sense that I was staring at her, like the time in the tent. She didn't seem to pick up on it, though. I contemplated on how, in the last seven days since I'd known her, I had never once seen her smile. I stared at her face, trying to imagine the corners of her mouth turned up, her eyes laughing. The image wouldn't come to me. Ellis gazed out across the lawn, her head propped on her arms. Except for the wind making the dark hair on the top of her head flutter, she was completely still. I hadn't seen her that way before—Ellis was always busy, always ready to tackle the next corner, making her plans. As I watched her, it occurred to me that Ellis wasn't simply serious. She was sad. Her broken heart was seeping out of every pore, wrapping itself around her like a grey shawl. It had been there all along, and I had never once noticed.

I sat up abruptly. Without lifting her head, Ellis raised her eyes and looked at me.

"Ellis," I began. "Why..."

"Hey, you two," my mother called, leaning in over the gate. "I want to come back and see what the two of you have done today."

Ellis got to her feet and unlatched the gate.

Mom walked into our little square of cleared wilderness and surveyed the tidy little patch we'd made.

"This is very nice. I can almost imagine the whole yard this way." She stepped out of her shoes and curled her toes in the grass. "Ahhh." She sighed.

"Hey, are those rose bushes?"

"Mr. Mosely is pruning them," Ellis told her.

"Mr. Mosely is?" Mom looked surprised.

"He came out for a while," I announced.

"Did he! Wow. You two are miracle workers."

I climbed to my feet and took her hand. "There's a surprise for you in the house."

"What is it?" she said, warily. "You didn't cook something, did you? Did you turn on the stove?"

What was with her? Why did she persist in thinking that I was destined to burn the house down?

"No," I protested in exasperation. "I didn't go near the stove." I tugged on her arm, pulling her towards the house.

"I have to go," Ellis said.

"Wait! No," I protested. "Come in with us."

"Grammy's waiting," Ellis replied. "I'll see you tomorrow."

I stood with my mother, watching Ellis head down the driveway. "It was Ellis's idea," I told her. "Now she won't even be here to see your face."

"I'm burning with curiosity," my mother said, with a hint of an edge in her voice. "You'd better show me what you've been up to."

I hesitated. What if she hated it? What if she got mad? Why did Ellis have to leave me alone with this? It had been her idea in the first place. Now, if Mom got mad, I'd have to bear the weight of her anger alone.

"Lead the way, Davy."

Heart in my throat, I went down the stairs. Mom followed until we were standing at her bedroom door.

"It's in my room?" she said, eyebrows arched. "You and Ellis were in my room?"

Whatever happened, done was done. I threw the door open and pulled my mother inside.

"Do you like it?" I screamed. I threw my hands over my mouth. I had not intended to yell, but nervousness and terror were wreaking havoc with my vocal cords.

Mom's eyes swept the room, falling on the flowers, the bedspread, the pictures, the curtains.

"Where," she finally managed to say, "did all this stuff come from?"

"Hannah's attic. It's old stuff that we cleaned up. She would've thrown it out otherwise. She wanted us to take it."

Mom went over to the bed and lowered herself onto the edge. I was in agony. Did she like it or hate it? Why wouldn't she say?

"Ellis and I painted the pictures."

Mom's eyes lingered over the pictures in their frames on the wall, and her fingers traced the new bedspread. She touched the cushions.

"We wanted you to have someplace nice."

Mom patted the spot beside her on the edge of the bed. I went to sit beside her.

"It is so nice," she said.

"You like it?" I breathed. "Really, you like it?" I exhaled with relief.

"It looks like a bedroom out of the Sears catalogue."

"Yeah, Ellis is good at that girly stuff," I agreed.

Mom fell back onto the bed and spread her arms out. "They've been good to us, Hannah and Ellis. Haven't they?"

I nodded and tipped backwards, lying beside her.

"Mom, did your house burn down when you were a kid?"

My mother laughed and rolled over onto her side to look at me. "No. Why are you asking such a crazy question?"

"You're always worried about me turning on the stove."

"Am I?" Mom looked surprised. "Well, I'm not worried about the house burning down as much as I am worried about you being hurt. Especially when

I'm not around. I wouldn't be able to forgive myself. Like that day at the pool, when you almost..."

The edges of her eyes turned silvery and wet, and she turned her head away. "I wish I could be here with you all the time."

"If wishes were horses." I smiled. "It's OK, Mom. You're doing your best."

Mom turned her face towards me. A teardrop dissolved into a slender fissure and made a hairline crack along her cheek.

"So are you, Davy. Don't think I haven't noticed."

"Mom, what if wishes were horses?"

"Beggars would ride," she replied. "It's an old saying. It means that life would be easy if we could have everything we wanted."

I tipped my face and stared at the ceiling. If there were any magical powers in the world, some genie or fairy or wizard that turned wishes into reality, I would never be so greedy as to ask for an entire herd of wish horses. I would just ask for one. Surely, pity would be taken on me if I limited myself to just one wish. This boy is not selfish like the others, the genies and fairies and wizards would concur. He has not asked for riches or toys or never-ending supplies of candy. Let us give him his one horse.

My wish would have a long dark mane and beautiful, sad grey eyes. She would stay near me always, rescuing me whenever I was in trouble. She would take me on her back and show me all the beautiful things I had never noticed before. We would find broken things and make them new. I would be kind to her and patient, and one day, I would see her eyes light up and hear her laugh. And there would be nothing that could ever separate us.

August, 1969

"It's the last week of summer holidays," Hannah said over lunch the next day. "I think the two of you have done enough work. I will have to insist that there is nothing but fun from this moment on. You'll be back to school next week. So I'm putting my foot down. The attic and the shed are off-limits. There will be no more gardening or decorating until further notice."

Ellis didn't look altogether pleased, but she nodded. She looked a little tired, I thought. My spirits were drooping as well, thinking about the end of the summer and of going back to school. Of Ellis's looming departure.

"What will we do for the rest of the week?" I called back as she pushed me in the tire swing.

"We could ride bikes. And Grammy said she'll take us to the beach one afternoon."

"I don't have a bike," I replied.

"You don't? Well, never mind. Grammy has a few in the shed. We'll just lower the seat on one of them." She caught the bottom of the swing and grasped it, and then ran through to the other side and let go. Under-doggie! I swooped backwards, hollering and laughing.

"I don't know how to ride a bike," I said as I sailed past her.

Ellis stopped pushing me and went to sit on

the porch steps. When the swing got low enough, I gathered my courage and leaped off, tumbling onto the grass. I scrambled to my feet and joined her.

"I'm going home on Friday," she said. "We've got three days. Can you learn how to ride a bike in three days?"

"I think so." I stuffed my fists into my eye sockets and rubbed hard. "Something in my eye," I mumbled.

"Davy," Ellis said gently. "We'll see each other again."

"I wish you didn't have to go," I blurted.

Ellis lifted her arm and draped it over my shoulders.

I leaned in a little, resting my head against her. I could hear the steady, gentle swish of her heart under her ribs. She smelled buttery and sweet, like Hannah's sugar cookies.

Present day

"So, were you any better at learning to ride a bike than you were at learning how to swim?" Will jokes. The two of us are out for breakfast, just tucking into our eggs and bacon and pancakes. I reach for a piece of toast and slather it with marmalade.

"Hey," I reply, "I could swim."

"Not much use when you can't do it in deep water." Will pours syrup over his pancakes. "You can stand up when you're in shallow water, Dad. You don't need to know how to swim for that."

I gave him a rueful look. "You don't do much for a person's self-esteem, you know?"

Will chuckles, and then takes a noisy swallow of his orange juice.

"To answer your question, I did learn how to ride a bike. It only took an afternoon. My knees and elbows got a little scraped up. The bike I practiced on didn't have training wheels. And no one wore helmets in those days. Still, I managed to avoid skull fractures and a concussion. A few months later, Grandpa bought me a new bike for my birthday. It was a wheelie bike with a banana seat, bright red. He and Grandma were already engaged by then."

"A wheelie bike?" Will shoves a whole slice of bacon into his mouth.

"Looked like a chopper. Long curvy handlebars and a long seat. Small wheels, good for popping wheelies."

"So, the wheel was invented by then?" Will snorts and slaps his napkin over his mouth.

I roll my eyes. "Yes, but the bike didn't have hand brakes."

"How'd you stop?"

"Pedalled backwards. That engaged the brake. It was a really cool bike. Best present I ever got when I was a kid."

"It would probably be a collector's item by now, if you'd kept it."

"Right," I agree ruefully. "Along with all the other antiques and artifacts of my distant childhood."

August, 1969

The last few days of that summer of 1969 are a blur in my mind—like a wet watercolour painting, with all the colours running into one another. The wind with its first edge of autumn crispness as Ellis and I raced bikes to the park. The sound of yelling and splashing coming from the public pool in the distance, the cloying sweet chill of grape popsicles as we rocked slowly back and forth on the swings. The mosaic pattern of sunlight in leaves as we lay in the grass beneath the trees. The slow path of the orbed sun across the sky the day Hannah took us to the beach. That was our last day.

The waves were high. As Hannah sat in her beach chair with her book, Ellis and I went out into water up to our waists to punch the waves.

Ellis would announce the impending arrival of the biggest ones, and we would plant our feet and raise our fists, fiercely and loudly daring the waves to try to knock us over. When the wave began to break over us, we would howl and threaten and pummel our fists into the crest, battling against the swell as it swept past. I laughed so much that my throat and chest ached. We staggered out of the water, blue-lipped and ravenous, and stuffed ourselves with sandwiches and potato chips. Our teeth crunched down on the grains of sand that always manage to make their way into beach picnic food.

Towards the end of the afternoon, Ellis and I constructed an elaborate sand castle, the ultimate in beautiful beach corners. We trimmed it with beach glass and smooth white stones and little sticks of worn driftwood. Hannah took our picture. She brought it over a few weeks later. I have it still. It's the only picture I have from that summer. We sit on either side of the castle, in black and white—Ellis looking at the camera through squinted, unsmiling eyes, with a strand of dark hair splayed across her face. Shoulders and chest bare, I kneel with my shaggy hair plastered to my forehead and one hand clutching the handle of a plastic pail. I'm not looking at the camera but at Ellis, with a sleepy half-smile. There are whitecaps behind us, undeterred in their endless rhythm in spite of the war we'd waged on them.

After we'd gone, the waves crept up behind our castle, pulling it down and away. It reverted back to granules of sand, and a litter of sticks and stones...

nothing left to show that it had been there at all.

We stopped for soft ice-cream on the way home. Hannah dropped us off at the top of my driveway. Ellis had slowly licked her ice cream into a soft peak at the top. I was already biting down into the recesses of the cone, almost finished. There was melted ice cream stuck to the tip of my nose.

"So," Ellis began.

I abruptly stopped gnawing on the cone. In my stomach, the ice-cream transformed instantly into a sour ball. I tossed the bottom of my cone into the sewer and felt the sudden, dropping weight of my sinking heart.

"Don't forget to move the frog every day for Mr. Mosely," Ellis instructed.

"I won't." The words stuck in my throat. My jaws ground together, and some stowaway grains of sand crunched gritty between my teeth. I looked at Ellis. Her face was calm, implacable. I felt the worst kind of despair working its way through me—the kind of despair you feel when you are worried that you love someone a whole hell of a lot more than they love you, and there's nothing you can do to change it.

"Grammy will write down my address for you," Ellis continued.

"I'm not much of a writer," I confessed. "I mean, I only just learned cursive last year. And I'm terrible at it." The prospect of sending Ellis my brutal attempts at letter-writing made me abjectly miserable. What could I possibly write to her? Grade Four is hard. My teacher is OK. Mom says hello. It was all so hollow and stupid and pointless. The things I wanted to say I could never find the courage for, or the words.

Ellis said nothing, just looked at me for a long moment. "I'll be back next summer, Davy."

"You'll be older," I said, my voice shrinking. I imagined Ellis, a year from now—fourteen years old, all the fading vestiges of her childhood totally vanished, not a remnant left. She'd graduate from corners to teenaged girl stuff, whatever that was. I didn't know, but I did understand that it would not likely include an eleven-year-old boy. The three-year gap between us seemed impassable. This was good-bye, in every sense of the word. Standing in front of me was an Ellis that I was never going to see again.

Ellis nodded and licked the edge of her cone, where rivulets of melted ice-cream were starting to run down.

"Gotta pack," she said. "See ya, Davy." She lifted her cone high in the air and bent to hug me with one arm. I didn't hug her back—the muscles in my arms and shoulders were clenching; I knew if I hugged her, it would be too hard, too desperate. She'd have to pry my arms off her. It would be humiliating.

I watched her walk down the driveway. A beach towel was draped over her bathing suit and her flip-flops scuffed against the pavement.

"Ellis," I called after her.

She stopped and turned half-way around. Her sober face looked back at me over her shoulder.

With every fibre of my being, I wanted to ask her. It was my last chance. I wanted to know what had happened to her, what it was that made her so sad. What it was that drove her to fix things up, to make them nice. Make them better.

She had made me better—even though she'd told me that she didn't think people could be fixed. She'd been wrong. Whatever happened at school the next week, it didn't matter so much. I had a friend in the world. And I could go on making corners. It almost made me double over admitting it, but I could make corners without her.

I couldn't find the words to tell her that. Or to ask the questions that had begun to plague me. And it was for the best. She'd been my friend, because I hadn't asked.

"I'll make a corner for you," I promised. "For when you come back."

"That would be just great." She lifted her chin then and brushed her hair away from her face. And then, for the briefest of moments, the corners of her mouth lifted, her eyes crinkled, and Ellis smiled.

Present day

"So," Will says, as he lays splayed across his unmade bed, comic books littered across his sheets. "I've never actually seen you swim in deep water, Dad. I have to wonder. Did you ever learn?"

"Of course, I did," I answer, and scoop to pluck his dirty soccer uniform off the floor. "All in good time. When I was ready. That's how kids learn."

"Dad." Will sighs. "It's the summer. Take off your teacher hat."

I laugh. "Hard to do. I've been wearing it for a long time."

Will smiles crookedly and sits up on his pillows. His dark hair is a riot of disheveled curls.

"And what about Mr. Mosely? Did the wandering frog cure him of agoraphobia?"

"When Grandma and I moved away, he was getting out into the yard more. He had most of the garbage and weeds cleared out. But I don't know what happened after that. We didn't stay in touch."

"I'll bet he got better. I'll bet he started going to the grocery store and for walks, maybe."

"Could be."

"And for haircuts. Hey, what about your haircut? Did Grandma take you to the barber before school started that year?"

I shook my head. "No. That was the last year I had to make do without the barber."

September, 1969

The day after Ellis left, my mother and I walked over to Hannah's. I dreaded going, being in the house without Ellis there. I imagined the house cold and silent, reeking of abandonment and loss. I imagined Hannah, sitting sadly in the front room, staring out the front window and blowing her nose.

We walked past the tire swing on our way to the front porch. It hung motionless from the rope, empty and forgotten. Impulsively, I shoved the tire with both hands, and it spiraled crookedly into the air, then knocked into the trunk of the tree. A red leaf fluttered down. I looked up and noticed the first flush of colour in the maples and the dry smell of musty leaves. Summer was over.

Hannah waved from her chair on the front porch. "I'm all ready for you," she called. "Coffee's on, Violet. Help yourself to a cup and I'll take care of David, here." Hannah seemed fine. Her usual cheerful self. I couldn't imagine how that was possible. I felt empty and lost. Like the sun had set inside me, and I was alone in the long darkness.

Mom squeezed Hannah's shoulder as she moved towards the front door. "How are you doing over here all by yourself?"

Hannah smiled. "It's quiet. But I'm fine. I'm good at filling my hours. I'm used to it."

"I miss Ellis already," Mom sighed, as she opened the screen door and went through. The smell of coffee wafted out in her wake.

Hannah stood and set her hands on my shoulders. "Hello there, David."

"Hi," I said.

We looked at one another, sadly. Hannah hugged me quickly then rubbed her hands together. "All right, then. Down to business. I've got a towel and scissors ready. Might as well get this over with. We'll get you looking spiffy for school on Tuesday."

"OK," I mumbled, unable to hide my lack of enthusiasm.

"Up you get," she said, gesturing at the stool she'd put out.

I climbed on and wound my feet around the legs. "Do you use a bowl?" I asked glumly. "When Mom cuts my hair, she puts a big bowl over my head and cuts off whatever hair is sticking out underneath."

Hannah laughed. "Well, that's one way to do it, but, no. No bowls involved, I promise." Hannah tied a towel around my neck and started to comb out my hair.

"Well, David. Good thing we're getting this job done. You'll be looking like one of the Beatles if this keeps up."

I started to hum Hey Jude through my gritted teeth.

"Bend your head," Hannah said. The scissors were cool against the back of my neck.

I raised my eyes and saw the doll house nearby. Ivy climbed up the stairs and out the windows of the little rooms.

"Why didn't Ellis put dolls or furniture in that doll house?" I said. "Why did she keep all that other stuff in there—rocks and glass and stuff?"

"Ellis was never one for dolls," Hannah said. "Keep your head down, just for another minute. Those things in the doll house—my daughter collected them when she was a young girl. The doll house was hers. Her daddy made it for her when she was four. He died the following year, in the Netherlands. During the war."

"Ellis made a special corner out of it," I said.

"Yes, she did," said Hannah. Her voice was different. Softer. "I kept all of those things that Kate collected. She had an eye for the most interesting little items. Always had her head down, scanning the ground for treasures. Kate—that was my daughter's name. She was Ellis's mother."

The scissors travelled across the nape of my neck. Snip, snip.

Was.

"She died, didn't she?"

Snip, snip. "Yes, David. She did." The comb moved through my hair.

"When did it happen?"

"Almost a year ago now," Hannah replied. "She had cancer."

"Ellis didn't tell me," I said.

"No, she wouldn't. Ellis doesn't talk about it at all. Not even to me. Not all summer."

"Why?"

Hannah came around in front of me and tilted my chin. Looking into my eyes, she smiled sadly. "People grieve in different ways Ellis makes corners. I think her corners are like memorials. That's the way she copes. Close your eyes. I'll trim your bangs."

"What's a memorial?" I said, clamping my eyes shut.

"It's something that people make, to remember someone. After my husband was killed, I made a scrapbook of all the photographs I had of him, and I wrote down all sorts of memories and funny things that had happened—and sad things, too. Good and bad. When someone dies, it's easy for people to forget the bad things and turn everything into flowers and butterflies. But I think it's important to remember everything about a person. If you only remember the good things, then you reinvent someone that never really existed. It's like losing them all over again. Nobody's perfect. We have to love the important people in our lives, just the way they are. Or were."

"Did you show the scrapbook to Ellis?"

"No. I will, someday. I'm working on another one for Kate. The scrapbooks are my memorials, for Caleb and for Kate. There. I'm finished."

I opened my eyes and looked down. The porch was littered with snarls of my sandy hair. A breeze wafted across the porch and the snarls drifted away like tumbleweeds. Gone forever.

Hannah passed me a hand-mirror, and I looked at myself in it. My hair looked great, just the way a barber would have done it. And it made me seem older somehow. But at that moment, I wasn't caring too much about my appearance.

"Did Ellis use Kate's room?"

"Yes," Hannah replied. "That was Kate's room, until she got married and moved away. I told Ellis she could use any of the bedrooms she wanted, but she asked for that one."

"She didn't want me to go in there."

"David, you're a young boy, and young boys have lots of questions. Ellis wasn't ready to talk about her mother. She needed to deal with it quietly, in her own way. And she was very particular about keeping things exactly the way Kate had left them. That bedroom was one spot she never considered turning into a corner."

"That's because it already was one."

"Very perceptive." Hannah nodded and shook the towel out over the porch rail. "Ellis needed some time away from home. That's why she spent the whole summer here with me. Her dad found someone else a few months ago. A really nice lady. They want to get married, and Ellis is finding it...hard. He thought some time away would do everyone some good."

"She could have just stayed here, then," I blurted.

"Why didn't she? She liked it here. And then you wouldn't have to be all alone."

Hannah helped me off the stool. "David, I love Ellis with all my heart, and I would love for her to live here with me. But that would be terribly selfish of me. Because it wouldn't be the best thing for Ellis. She needs to face things, not hide from them. She needs to move on with her life, and she needs to understand that her father has to do the same. Before she started spending time with you, she was upstairs far too much. I talked her into going to the pool, into helping with the garden, coming with me to church...but what she really wanted was to go in that room, close the door, and look through all the drawers and boxes, and read her mother's old books. She's a good girl and would do everything I asked, but...I was terribly worried for her. I would check on her through the night, and she would be laying there in the dark, wide awake. I'm just not sleepy, she would explain. Don't worry about me, Grammy. But I was worried. Worried sick. Until that evening you and your mother showed up at my door. It was the best thing that could have happened for Ellis."

"All this time, I thought she was helping me," I said.

Mom came out onto the porch with her coffee, and exclaimed over my haircut. "My God, Davy! You look two years older!" She bent down so that our faces were level and beamed at me. I squirmed.

"They grow up so fast," Mom said to Hannah.

Hannah nodded. "Don't they, though?"

Between then and now

I didn't see Ellis again the next year, nor for many years after that. My mother and Gabe were married the following spring, and we were gone by the time Ellis returned to Hannah's house for her summer stay. Mom often talked about making the three-hour drive back there for a visit, but it never happened. Between being pregnant with my three sisters and dealing with babies and toddlers and domestic calamities, the years just got away. Mom and Hannah remained friends, speaking often by telephone. There was often news of Ellis as she grew up—her progress in high school, her acceptance into university, her first job. Her father had remarried by the end of 1969, and Ellis had a new brother the following year. She was fine, from all reports.

Ellis and I did exchange letters that first year or so—regularly, at first. She was far better at it than I. My letters weren't even letters, just brief notes, stuffed in with various drawings I'd made for her. Once I was eleven, sending drawings to a fourteen-year-old girl seemed uncool, so I stopped.

Still, all was not lost. As I grew up, Ellis's corners stuck to me—following me into the back yard, where I'd make special play spots for my sisters; into my new room, where I turned the roll-top desk into a drawing corner. When I grew up, my interest in art led me to university, where I got a degree in Art

History, and then to Teachers' College. I've taught high school art for several years. My classroom studio is a corner room, with windows on two sides. The light is perfect for drawing, and there are views over the football field all the way back to the woods. I've worked hard to make my corner room appealing and inspiring to the kids. The walls are filled with pieces kids have left behind when they moved on—still-lifes, abstracts, landscapes, collages, and portraits. The Starry Night chair has found a permanent home in the back corner. (Mr. Mosely let me take it with me when I moved). I still sit in it and sketch sometimes, over a lunch break when I need some quiet or at the end of a school day, to de-stress. The shelves at the back of the room are crammed with a mishmash of supplies—glues, oil pastels, empty yogurt containers, paints and brushes, and scraps of fabric and specialty papers. I've got a pretty good sound system in there. The kids like to work to music. I give them a good mix of classical, jazz, rock, pop, and occasionally, some sixties tunes, just to round it all out. I'm proud of my corner. I think it's one of my best.

In the summer of 1984, shortly after I'd obtained my teaching position, my mother called one evening.

"Hannah Greary passed away," she told me. "She was in the hospital after a mild heart attack. She had a massive one the next day."

I hadn't seen Hannah since 1970, but the news hit me hard.

"We'll go to the visitation, Mom. Both of us?"

"Yes. We should. I want to."

"Me, too."

As we drove along the highway the following afternoon, Mom and I relived a lot of our memories of that last summer before we'd moved away. Mom still used the enormous ceramic pie plate Hannah had given to her as a wedding gift. And she still kept the chipped jug on her kitchen table that Ellis and I had found in the attic. Hannah had knit sweater and bootie sets for each of the girls and sent them to Mom when they were born. We recalled Hannah's sugar cookies and her cinnamon buns, her enormous vegetable garden, and her welcoming front porch. We reflected on Hannah's inherent kindness, how it seemed to radiate so naturally from her.

Mom shook her head. "I don't know, Davy. I find kindness to be such a lot of work. It's worth it, but it doesn't always come easily. For Hannah, it seemed effortless. She was more of a mother to me in two weeks than my own mother was in seventeen years."

The parking lot at the funeral home was packed. I had to leave the car on a side street. Mom took my arm and we walked silently up the street and joined the line.

We waited for almost an hour before we got to the receiving line. The coffin was white and covered in a spray of yellow roses. And closed. I sighed inwardly with relief. I have never understood the custom of an open coffin, the make-up and the carefully styled hair, the folded waxy hands. An honest photograph is infinitely preferable to the shell-shock of seeing someone once familiar and beloved turned to something so unrecognizable. There was a recent photograph of Hannah on the coffin lid—her hair completely white and a few more lines in her face—but Hannah, in her essence, wearing her apron and standing on her front porch.

I shook hands with a man around my mother's age. "I'm Alan Wynne," he told me. "Hannah was my late wife's mother."

"I'm sorry for your loss. I'm David. You're Ellis's father?"

"That's right. You know Ellis?"

"A long time ago. She was my babysitter one

summer when she was staying with Hannah."

Mr. Wynne pondered for a moment, his forehead creasing, and then his face brightened. "Davy?"

"That's me," I nodded. "This is my mother, Violet Blanchard. She and Hannah were friends."

Alan shook my mother's hand. "Ellis has told us so much about the two of you! How good of you to come. Ellis will be so glad to see you. She's down a little further, at the end of the line."

I craned my neck, but the room was so full of people that I couldn't even catch a glimpse of her.

"Hannah was a special lady," my mother said to Alan. "She was so good to us."

Alan smiled. "I've heard that a lot today."

There was a veritable crowd waiting behind us to pay their respects, so we moved on, past others who introduced themselves as Hannah's nieces, cousins, sisters. My mother lingered to speak to one of Hannah's sisters, and I moved on alone.

And there she was. Ellis. Wearing a simple black dress and heels. Her dark hair was still long, falling thick over her shoulders. All grown up, and so beautiful. I felt the shock in my stomach, as though I had just bolted down a very large glass of ice water.

I took her hands in mine, and she looked up at me with her solemn grey eyes.

"Davy Barowsky," she said. "You're taller than me."

"It's so great to see you, Ellis," I said. "And it's Blanchard, now. Gabe adopted me when I was eleven."

"And your voice has changed."

I laughed. "I'm twenty-five." We stood there, holding hands, searching one another's faces.

"I heard that Gabe adopted you," Ellis finally said. "That's really great."

"It sure is," I agreed. "He's been good to me."

"Remember when I saved your life?" she teased.

Her eyes lifted a little at the corners.

"I do, as a matter of fact. And thanks again, for that." My eyes began to sting a little, and I blinked, hard. "I'm sorry, Ellis. About Hannah..."

Ellis nodded and moved in closer. Her arms circled around my back, and her head dropped against my shoulder. I held her, carefully. All the hairs on my arms were standing up, like they had that day in the centre of the lilac bush. I glanced quickly beside her, to see if there was anyone standing in the husband or boyfriend spot. There wasn't.

"After you and Violet moved away, Grammy went over to Mr. Mosely's every so often. Did you know that? To move the frog."

"She did?" I cleared my throat and tried not to snuffle. "Of course, she did," I answered myself. "That's not surprising at all." Reluctantly, I moved my arms away from her, and we stepped apart. Both of our faces were wet.

"Remember that night we had the campout, and I hid the Aspirin because I wanted to keep us away from that girl who had polio? I thought we were going to catch it."

Ellis shook her head, confused. "You hid the Aspirin?"

Hannah had kept her word. She'd never told Ellis my embarrassing story.

"Ellis," my mother exclaimed softly. "My God, look at you." The two women embraced. Mom stood back, holding Ellis's shoulders. "The last time Hannah and I spoke on the phone, she said you might be getting engaged."

My chest tightened a little, but I smiled quickly. "That's wonderful. Congratulations."

"That didn't work out," Ellis said. Her face flushed a little under the tears.

"Oh, God. I'm sorry," my mother fumbled.

"Please, don't worry about it. It was for the best, believe me."

I took my mother's elbow. "There are people waiting behind us," I whispered. "We should move on."

"Are you going to be in town for a while?" Ellis ventured. "Maybe you could come over tomorrow? The funeral's not until the day after. I'm staying at Grammy's with my dad and step-mom and my brother. We could visit some more, catch up a bit?"

"We certainly are," my mother replied. "I'll call you later."

Mom and I walked back to the car.

"I thought we had to get back," I said. "You said you have an appointment in the morning."

Mom slipped the seatbelt over her shoulder. "Ellis is beautiful, don't you think? Even prettier than Hannah described her. And she's an interior designer, very successful. She has her own business. Not too far from where we live."

"You never mentioned that," I replied. Interior design. That made sense. Corners everywhere, and Ellis was paid for them to boot.

"Didn't I? I thought I had."

"Nope, you didn't."

"We'll find a hotel and have breakfast at Cookie's tomorrow."

"Is that place still around?"

"New owner, same place. It hasn't changed much, from what Hannah told me. Cookie retired several years back. Moved to Florida and got married."

"You never told me that, either."

"Davy, I wish you would stop reprimanding me." Mom scowled at me.

"If wishes were horses." I shrugged.

Mom gave me a sharp look, and then laughed. "That's what kids do to you when they grow up. They turn around and use your own words against you."

"I'm ordering a milkshake for breakfast," I informed her. "And you know what else? I turn on my stove. All the time."

Present day

Early morning, Will comes into our bedroom. "Sam's on the phone," he announces. The corners of his mouth are smeared with peanut butter. He goes back out, closing the door behind him.

I groan, roll over, and peer at the clock on the night stand. "It's only seven o'clock," I protest. All three of our boys defied the odds and grew up to be early risers. I grope for the phone.

"Hey, Sam," I say. "It's early."

"I was up at six, Dad. I wanted to call you then." Sam chuckles.

"I suppose I should thank you?" I yawn.

"You will, when you hear my news. Chrissie and I are getting married."

I sit bolt upright in the bed. "You're...she..."

Sam chuckles again. "Put Mom on. I can't trust you with the details."

I reach out, find the curve of Ellis's hip, which is warm and still under the sheet. "Wake up," I say, prodding her. "Sam's on the phone. He has something to tell you."

Ellis whimpers a little and opens her eyes a fraction. "This had better be good," she croaks.

"Oh, it's good," I assure her.

I sit up in the bed, thrust a couple pillows behind me, and watch Ellis's face as she takes in the news. Sam and Chrissie had met in university in Sam's second year. Chrissie had been at our house for every Thanksgiving, Christmas, and Easter dinner ever since.

"Where did you propose? Did you set a date? Have you told Chrissie's parents? Have you talked about a theme? You'll let me help, won't you? I'm a details person, Sam... No, I won't take over! I don't plan on being that kind of mother-in-law! All right. See you soon."

Ellis flops across my stomach and flings the phone onto the nightstand.

"They're coming for supper. And they're picking up Cooper and his new girlfriend on the way. You'd better call Violet and Gabe and invite them," Ellis says while pushing her hair out of her eyes so that she can look at me. Her grey eyes are filled with sparkle.

"House full again," I say, smoothing a rogue tendril of hair away from her face with my index finger. Since her forties, Ellis hasn't worn her hair as long as she used to. She keeps it in a shoulder-length bob now and goes to great length and expense to keep it dark.

"No greys in this corner," she avows.

"Next thing you know, we'll be calling you Grammy," I say, as I run my thumb along the curve of her cheek. She has these beautiful little smile lines around her eyes now. Smile lines.

Ellis's face glows. "This family needs a Grammy," she says, and plants a kiss on my cheek. "Ouch. Prickly." She rolls off the bed and flounces into the bathroom. "Not to mention a Grampy. So many plans to make," she calls from behind the door.

The shower turns on and the singing begins. My wife has many, many talents. Singing is not one of them. I shift down in the bed, sprawling in the sheets, luxuriating in the warmth where Ellis had just been, sleeping beside me.

In the shower, the caterwauling begins with the opening lines of Blue Suede's "Hooked on a Feeling." One of her favourites. I grimace and bury my face in her pillow. My hands search around, looking for another one to put over my ears.

God, she is awful. The pillow over my ears isn't helping at all. I sit up, swing my legs over the edge of the bed, and then dart out the bedroom door.

Will is sprawled on the couch in the family room, watching cartoons and shoveling vast quantities of cereal up towards his face. I open my mouth, about to spill the good news, but then clamp it shut again. I should let Sam tell him. I walk past Will to the patio doors and slip outside.

The yard is saturated with dew, the early morning swollen with birdsong. Colours blossom in all the corners; the flowers I'd planted were at their summer peak. A robin alights on the bird bath, sending sprays of silvery water shooting out from all sides as it soaks its feathers. The corner beds in the yard are ones I'd made for Ellis. They are to make up for the corner I'd promised her at the end of the summer of 1969—a promise, as it turned out, I hadn't been able to keep.

Over on the clothesline, a solitary blouse hangs forgotten and adrift in the breeze, its empty arms filling with wind. Shivering, I walk barefoot through the wet grass, remove the clothespins, and gather the blouse in my arms. It smells amazing, like sunshine, wind, and something slightly citrus; a lingering perfume, the scent of wife. My Ellis, with a short e. Life-saver. Mermaid. Pusher of tire swings and master of under-doggies. Gatherer of flowers, gleaner of attics. Encourager of the agoraphobic. Beautiful, dark-maned wish horse. Filler of empty corners.

Especially mine.

The End

About the Author

Corrina Austin is a retired elementary school teacher, living in beautiful South-Western Ontario, Canada. She has Bachelor's degrees in both English and Education. Corrina has published several short stories and essays and was twice the recipient of grants for a novel in progress from the Ontario Arts Council. "Corners" was inspired by her experiences as a child growing up in the 1960's and contains many artifacts from her memories of those times. To get to know her better, check out her blog at www.trustcake.wordpress.com. You can also visit her on Twitter (@corrinaaustin), Instagram (readingcorners) and via her author page on Facebook.